ANN

NURSERY TEA AND POISON

ANNE Morice, *née* Felicity Shaw, was born in Kent in 1916.

Her mother Muriel Rose was the natural daughter of Rebecca Gould and Charles Morice. Muriel Rose married a Kentish doctor, and they had a daughter, Elizabeth. Muriel Rose's three later daughters—Angela, Felicity and Yvonne—were fathered by playwright Frederick Lonsdale.

Felicity's older sister Angela became an actress, married actor and theatrical agent Robin Fox, and produced England's Fox acting dynasty, including her sons Edward and James and grandchildren Laurence, Jack, Emilia and Freddie.

Felicity went to work in the office of the GPO Film Unit. There Felicity met and married documentarian Alexander Shaw. They had three children and lived in various countries.

Felicity wrote two well-received novels in the 1950's, but did not publish again until successfully launching her Tessa Crichton mystery series in 1970, buying a house in Hambleden, near Henley-on-Thames, on the proceeds. Her last novel was published a year after her death at the age of seventy-three on May 18th, 1989.

BY ANNE MORICE
and available from Dean Street Press

ANNE MORICE

NURSERY TEA AND POISON

With an introduction and afterword by
Curtis Evans

DEAN STREET PRESS

INTRODUCTION

BY 1970 the Golden Age of detective fiction, which had dawned in splendor a half-century earlier in 1920, seemingly had sunk into shadow like the sun at eventide. There were still a few old bodies from those early, glittering days who practiced the fine art of finely clued murder, to be sure, but in most cases the hands of those murderously talented individuals were growing increasingly infirm. Queen of Crime Agatha Christie, now eighty years old, retained her bestselling status around the world, but surely no one could have deluded herself into thinking that the novel *Passenger to Frankfurt*, the author's 1970 "Christie for Christmas" (which publishers for want of a better word dubbed "an Extravaganza") was prime Christie—or, indeed, anything remotely close to it. Similarly, two other old crime masters, Americans John Dickson Carr and Ellery Queen (comparative striplings in their sixties), both published detective novels that year, but both books were notably weak efforts on their parts. Agatha Christie's American counterpart in terms of work productivity and worldwide sales, Erle Stanley Gardner, creator of Perry Mason, published nothing at all that year, having passed away in March at the age of eighty. Admittedly such old-timers as Rex Stout, Ngaio Marsh, Michael Innes and Gladys Mitchell were still playing the game with some of their old élan, but in truth their glory days had fallen behind them as well. Others, like Margery Allingham and John Street, had died within the last few years or, like Anthony Gilbert, Nicholas Blake, Leo Bruce and Christopher Bush, soon would expire or become debilitated. Decidedly in 1970—a year which saw the trials of the Manson family and the Chicago Seven, assorted bombings, kidnappings and plane hijackings by such terroristic entities as the Weathermen, the Red Army, the PLO and the FLQ, the American invasion of Cambodia and the Kent State shootings and the drug overdose deaths of Jimi Hendrix and Janis Joplin—leisure readers now more than ever stood in need of the intelligent escapism which classic crime fiction provided. Yet the old order in crime fiction, like that in world politics and society, seemed irrevocably to be washing away in a bloody tide of violent anarchy and all round uncouthness.

Or was it? Old values have a way of persisting. Even as the generation which produced the glorious detective fiction of the Golden Age finally began exiting the crime scene, a new generation of younger puzzle adepts had arisen, not to take the esteemed places of their elders, but to contribute their own worthy efforts to the rarefied field of fair play murder. Among these writers were P.D. James, Ruth Rendell, Emma Lathen, Patricia Moyes, H.R.F. Keating, Catherine Aird, Joyce Porter, Margaret Yorke, Elizabeth Lemarchand, Reginald Hill, Peter Lovesey and the author whom you are perusing now, Anne Morice (1916-1989). Morice, who like Yorke, Lovesey and Hill debuted as a mystery writer in 1970, was lavishly welcomed by critics in the United Kingdom (she was not published in the United States until 1974) upon the publication of her first mystery, *Death in the Grand Manor*, which suggestively and anachronistically was subtitled not an "extravaganza," but a novel of detection. Fittingly the book was lauded by no less than seemingly permanently retired Golden Age stalwarts Edmund Crispin and Francis Iles (aka Anthony Berkeley Cox). Crispin deemed Morice's debut puzzler "a charming whodunit . . . full of unforced buoyance" and prescribed it as a "remedy for existentialist gloom," while Iles, who would pass away at the age of seventy-seven less than six months after penning his review, found the novel a "most attractive lightweight," adding enthusiastically: "[E]ntertainingly written, it provides a modern version of the classical type of detective story. I was much taken with the cheerful young narrator . . . and I think most readers will feel the same way. Warmly recommended." Similarly, Maurice Richardson, who, although not a crime writer, had reviewed crime fiction for decades at the *London Observer*, lavished praise upon Morice's maiden mystery: "Entrancingly fresh and lively whodunit. . . . Excellent dialogue. . . . Much superior to the average effort to lighten the detective story."

With such a critical sendoff, it is no surprise that Anne Morice's crime fiction took flight on the wings of its bracing mirth. Over the next two decades twenty-five Anne Morice mysteries were published (the last of them post-humously), at the rate of one or two year. Twenty-three of these concerned the investigations of Tessa Crichton, a charming young actress who always manages to cross paths with murder, while two, written at the end of her career, detail cases of Detective Superintendent "Tubby" Wiseman. In 1976 Morice along with Margaret Yorke was chosen to become a member of Britain's prestigious Detection Club, preceding Ruth Rendell by a year, while in the 1980s her books were included in Bantam's superlative paperback "Murder Most British" series, which included luminaries from both present and past like Rendell, Yorke, Margery Allingham, Patricia Wentworth, Christianna Brand, Elizabeth Ferrars, Catherine Aird, Margaret Erskine, Marian Babson, Dorothy Simpson, June Thomson and last, but most certainly not least, the Queen of Crime herself, Agatha Christie. In 1974, when Morice's fifth Tessa Crichton detective novel, *Death of a Dutiful Daughter*, was picked up in the United States, the author's work again was received with acclaim, with reviewers emphasizing the author's cozy traditionalism (though the term "cozy" had not then come into common use in reference to traditional English and American mysteries). In his notice of Morice's *Death of a Wedding Guest* (1976), "Newgate Callendar" (aka classical music critic Harold C. Schoenberg), Seventies crime fiction reviewer for the *New York Times Book Review*, observed that "Morice is a traditionalist, and she has no surprises [in terms of subject matter] in her latest book. What she does have, as always, is a bright and amusing style . . . [and] a general air of sophisticated writing." Perhaps a couple of reviews from Middle America—where intense Anglophilia, the dogmatic pronouncements of Raymond Chandler and Edmund Wilson notwithstanding, still ran rampant among mystery readers—best indicate the cozy criminal appeal of Anne Morice:

> Anne Morice . . . acquired me as a fan when I read her "Death and the Dutiful Daughter." In this new novel, she did not disappoint me. The same appealing female detective, Tessa Crichton, solves the mysteries on her own, which is surprising in view of the fact that Tessa is actually not a detective, but a film actress. Tessa just seems to be at places where a murder occurs, and at the most unlikely places at that . . . this time at a garden fete on the estate of a millionaire tycoon. . . . The plot is well constructed; I must confess that I, like the police, had my suspect all picked out too. I was "dead" wrong (if you will excuse the expression) because my suspect was

also murdered before not too many pages turned. ... This is not a blood-curdling, chilling mystery; it is amusing and light, but Miss Morice writes in a polished and intelligent manner, providing pleasure and entertainment. (Rose Levine Isaacson, review of *Death of a Heavenly Twin*, *Jackson Mississippi Clarion-Ledger*, 18 August 1974)

I like English mysteries because the victims are always rotten people who deserve to die. Anne Morice, like Ngaio Marsh et al., writes tongue in cheek but with great care. It is always a joy to read English at its glorious best. (Sally Edwards, "Ever-So British, This Tale," review of *Killing with Kindness*, *Charlotte North Carolina Observer*, 10 April 1975)

While it is true that Anne Morice's mysteries most frequently take place at country villages and estates, surely the quintessence of modern cozy mystery settings, there is a pleasing tartness to Tessa's narration and the brittle, epigrammatic dialogue which reminds me of the Golden Age Crime Queens (particularly Ngaio Marsh) and, to part from mystery for a moment, English playwright Noel Coward. Morice's books may be cozy but they most certainly are not cloying, nor are the sentiments which the characters express invariably "traditional." The author avoids any traces of soppiness or sentimentality and has a knack for clever turns of phrase which is characteristic of the bright young things of the Twenties and Thirties, the decades of her own youth. "Sackcloth and ashes would have been overdressing for the mood I had sunk into by then," Tessa reflects at one point in the novel *Death in the Grand Manor*. Never fear, however: nothing, not even the odd murder or two, keeps Tessa down in the dumps for long; and invariably she finds herself back on the trail of murder most foul, to the consternation of her handsome, debonair husband, Inspector Robin Price of Scotland Yard (whom she meets in the first novel in the series and has married by the second), and the exasperation of her amusingly eccentric and indolent playwright cousin, Toby Crichton, both of whom feature in almost all of the Tessa Crichton novels. Murder may not lastingly mar Tessa's equanimity, but she certainly takes her detection seriously.

Three decades now having passed since Anne Morice's crime novels were in print, fans of British mystery in both its classic and cozy forms should derive much pleasure in discovering (or rediscovering) her work in these new Dean Street Press editions and thereby passing time once again in that pleasant fictional English world where death affords us not emotional disturbance and distress but enjoyable and intelligent diversion.

Curtis Evans

CHAPTER ONE

1

NOT everything my parents did or attempted to do for me met with my unqualified approval, but I have always considered that in appointing Serena Hargrave as chief godmother they made the right move.

Despite her own frustrated and disappointing life, with its single halcyon period in her early twenties, she had never once forgotten me at Christmas or on my birthday, had rallied cheerfully to the bedside through measles and whooping cough and, with a sacrifice which only later got through to me, had regularly taken me out from school, to ply me with exotic food and listen to vainglorious and utterly tedious accounts of my performance in the school play. Moreover, these kind attentions had continued even after she married and had a daughter of her own and during her subsequent widowhood and comparative penury.

It was true that in recent years she had shown a tendency to become strict and unbending in her attitudes, as well as compulsively tidy, but I considered this to be excusable, given her age and circumstances, and it did not detract one jot from my regard and affection. So it was a genuine sorrow to be obliged to quibble when she telephoned one Thursday evening to invite Robin and me to spend the following weekend at her cottage in Herefordshire.

'I'm terribly sorry, Serena, but I don't see how we can. Robin has to go and help out with some case in the Midlands. He's leaving tomorrow morning.'

'That's a shame, Tessa, but I can't pretend that I seriously expected him to drop everything at a minute's notice, just to suit me. Can't you come on your own, or are you still caught up in that television series?'

'No, they finished shooting that last week; it's the problem of transport mainly, you being about a hundred miles from a railway station. Robin will be taking the car.'

'My goodness, Tessa, aren't our Detective Inspectors provided with official cars for these purposes?'

'Usually they are, but this time he wants to drive up under his own steam and use official transport when he gets to the scene. I'm not sure why. Something to do with this passion for being independent, I suppose.'

'Whereabouts in the Midlands, exactly?'

'Can't remember, Serena. All I know is that it has to do with some crash on one of the motorways.'

'There now! And he once got so cross with me for not understanding that the C.I.D. or whatever they call themselves had no connection with the traffic police.'

'Yes, that's true, but you see when they had this crash the other day it turned out that a man who had been found in the driving seat of one of the cars was dead when they got him to the hospital and some gimlet eyed doctor noticed that his injuries weren't compatible with that kind of accident. So now they think he was put in the car when he was already dead and the real driver engineered this little pile up, switched places with the corpse and then escaped in the general confusion. Quite a smart way of disposing of it, in a sense, only it hasn't altogether worked out and Robin has been flung into the breach to try and ensure that it doesn't.'

'What a vile story! Which motorway did it happen on?'

'The M.6, I think.'

'Oh well, that's all right then.'

'I'm not with you, Serena. How can that make it all right?'

'Oh, not the horrid crime, I don't mean that, but there's a turn off from the M.6 not more than ten miles from here, and surely dear, kind Robin wouldn't object to making a small detour to drop you off? There are two cars here at present, so no problem about getting you to the station for the fast train on Monday, if he can't collect you.'

'Okay, I can but ask him.'

'Yes, do, there's a dear. I don't want to sound selfish, but I really do need some moral support, someone neutral who's outside the family, if you see what I mean?'

'Why? Is there a war on?'

Serena laughed: 'That's what I'm trying to avoid.'

I became rather thoughtful on hearing this, because although I have played a few funny parts in my time, both on and off the screen, up till then the role of peacemaker had not been among them. Misconstruing my silence and evidently regarding the matter as settled, Serena began on her thanks and goodbyes, but I cut in just in time to say:

'Hang on a minute, Serena. What's all this about? For instance, whose car shall I be conveyed to the station in on Monday morning?'

'Well, you'll never believe this, Tessa, but I'm afraid the answer is Pelham's.'

'Pelham? You mean he's in England?'

'Yes, and been staying here for over a week. Not only Pelham, I might add, but his new American bride as well.'

'You stagger me! I didn't even know he had one.'

'Neither did we, until the day before they landed on us. It has sent Primrose into the full sulks, as you might have predicted, so she's no help; and Nannie is worse than useless these days. Also I have the impression that Pelham doesn't entirely approve of Jake as a tenant, and a new American bride is another thing I could very easily do without at present, so, one way and another, matters have reached a rather tricky stage.'

'I can imagine! I expect I'd have come anyway, but if you'd told me all this at the beginning Hell and high water wouldn't have stopped me.'

She laughed again: 'And to think I was afraid of scaring you off!'

'Not a chance in the world. Expect me when you see me, if not sooner.'

2

'Rather a modest exaggeration, on the whole,' Robin admitted, when I put the proposal to him that evening. 'Time and distance being elastic, so far as women are concerned.'

'Does all that mean that the M.6 doesn't go anywhere near?'

'Well, perhaps not quite so near as it suited her to make out. As I remember, the motorway is about six miles east of Ross, and Serena's village another eight miles west again. However, I daresay I can accommodate you, if you can be ready to leave by eleven. I've one or two things to clear up at this end first and I'd like to get to Wolverhampton not later than four. Who's Pelham, anyway?'

'Serena's brother-in-law. Surely you remember Pelham? In a way, his was the oddest part of the whole story. I must have told you.'

'I expect you have, but it was all so long ago. You'll have to tell me again.'

'I will, but not tonight. You look tired and it'll do very nicely to while away our journey tomorrow.'

'Oh no, it won't. Sergeant Brook will be with us.'

'What does that matter? I should think he would find it quite entertaining.'

'Maybe he would, on some different occasion. Tomorrow he'll be expecting me to concentrate on the here and now.'

'Well, as to that,' I said, 'there are two ways of looking at it. The first part of the Hargrave story may be over and done with, but it sounds to me as though the next chapter had already begun and I daresay it will turn out to be quite as fascinating, in its minor key way, as your old murder on the M.6.'

'No takers,' Robin said. 'You could well be right. Specially now that you're about to take a hand in it. We'll have to compare notes on Monday.'

CHAPTER TWO

PELHAM Hargrave, as I was unable to remind Robin on our journey north, had been born the younger of twin brothers and thus, with a lack of opportunism which was to characterise him in later life, had forfeited by half an hour his claim to a large estate, including manor house and park and a vast private income. All these benefits had accrued instead to his brother, Rupert, who for a brief period had been Serena's husband and who hardly needed them at all, having also been endowed with sufficient brains, energy and application to have earned him all the material assets he could want.

Their parents had been killed in a car crash in Spain when they were six years old and Rupert's inheritance had come to him directly from his grandfather, the founder of a shipping firm, thereby presenting him with another unearned bonus, for it seems there is great financial advantage in skipping over a whole generation and acquiring property while still a minor.

After their grandfather's death only a year or two later, the estate had been administered. jointly by an agent and a firm of solicitors, but the management of the house and the boys' upbringing had stayed almost exclusively in the hands of the nurse who had looked after them as babies. Various female relatives, inspired by altruistic or predatory motives, had attempted to wrest some of this power from her, but none had succeeded. The weaker among them had capitulated with barely a struggle and such braver members who had stood up to her rudeness and hostility had swiftly found Rupert and Pelham ranged solidly against them and themselves operating in a kind of cold war, having all their proposals met with dumb insolence and eating solitary meals in the dining room as they listened to the shouts of laughter coming from the nursery.

In relating all this to me, Serena had added that to Nannie, Rupert, in particular, had been above criticism and that she had spoilt him unmercifully. Had it not been for his accident, his character must have been permanently ruined by her ignorant and misguided indulgence.

The accident in question had not appeared to contain mitigating features at the time, except insofar as it had not been fatal. It had occurred during a pheasant shoot soon after the boys' last term at school and a few weeks before they were both due to go up to Oxford, and as a result of it Rupert had lost his right eye.

This would have been a deep misfortune for any eighteen-year-old boy, but the effect on Rupert, who had never known misfortune in his life, was catastrophic. Although enduring the physical pain with courage and stoicism, mentally he fell to pieces under the ordeal, becoming moody and bitter and in an almost constant state of irritability, and curiously enough Pelham was almost as bad. As though literally sharing his twin's suffering, his response to it had followed the identical pattern. Since Rupert was unable to take up his place at Oxford, Pelham refused to go either, but loped about the house and grounds, snarling at anyone who dared to approach him and flatly declining either to study or to take any part in running the estate.

It was not known who had fired the shot which caused all this agony, or possibly known only to Rupert, which amounted to the same thing, for he refused to be interrogated on the subject, or even to allow a mention of it in his presence.

This state of affairs lasted for several years and even Nannie wilted under the strain, her splendid domination gradually becoming eroded by her beloved charges' withdrawal from herself and from everyone around them. Although they did not cease to cosset and protect her, the old cosy intimacy had gone and by the time Rupert became engaged to be married her rule had so far declined as to make her attempts to upset this apple cart so querulous and ineffectual that even the faint hearted Serena was not seriously troubled by them.

Rupert was twenty-four by then and his outlook had improved even before he re-met and fell in love with Serena, his childhood friend and daughter of the village doctor, herself an orphan by then. He had refused to try again for the university, but two or three years after his accident had entered the family business, succeeding remarkably well in it, by all accounts. No one was particularly surprised by this because he was ambitious by nature, as well as clever, but the real surprise was provided by Pelham.

For once, he declined to follow in his brother's footsteps and during this period remained at home and mooned about as before. Then, on the day after Rupert became engaged, Pelham, with no previous warning and with only a pittance to call his own, had declared his intention of emigrating to Canada. A fortnight later he was gone and for several years, apart from an occasional postcard, nothing more was heard of him. Eventually the news filtered through that he had transferred himself from British Columbia to California, but he had never returned to his native land, nor evinced the slightest desire to do so.

Rupert's marriage lasted for three years and was an ideally happy one. Although with rehabilitation he had regained much of his former arrogance and could on occasions be rude and overbearing, Serena remained unwavering in her devotion and I have been told that, so long as he was getting his own way, no one could have been more agreeable and attractive.

Just before their third anniversary Serena discovered that she was pregnant, which was a great joy and relief to them both, but on the following Sunday evening it was Rupert who was stricken by severe abdominal pains. He was taken to the local cottage hospital for an emergency operation for what appeared to be an acute appendicitis and within three days had died from peritonitis. It transpired that a minute fragment of the shot which had entered his eye had become lodged in his intestines and after staying dormant for nearly ten years had finally killed him.

I was too young at the time for these events to make any deep impression on me, but Serena has told me since that she drifted through the subsequent months in a state of semi-oblivion and total rootlessness. Not only had she lost her beloved husband, but with his death her entire future, position in life, security and well-being depended solely on the sex of the unborn child, since everything was entailed on the eldest surviving son. At the end of six months Primrose was born and Pelham became the owner of Chargrove Manor, with fourteen thousand acres and an income to match them. By the same stroke, Serena was rendered homeless, with only her tiny marriage settlement on which to live and bring up her daughter.

Cables had been despatched to Pelham both before and after his brother's death, but he had ignored them, signifying in a letter to Serena a few months later that nothing that had happened made him more inclined to return to England, and at this point Nannie had come into her own again, rising like a phoenix from the ashes and swooping down on her new prey. With incredible prescience, she insisted on taking over full charge of Primrose, whom she thereafter referred to as 'my baby's baby', of making all her clothes and knitting all her shawls and blankets, for no remuneration whatever, and furthermore declared her intention of remaining with the family and working her fingers to the bone for them, even if it meant living in two rooms and paying the rent out of her own savings.

Too desolate and confused to see where all this would lead, Serena had been swept along in the whirlwind, allowing Nannie full rein and the gradual usurpation of all her former power, although in the event the drastic sacrifices proved to be unnecessary. When eventually submitting to the demands of trustees and others to make some settlement of his affairs, Pelham behaved quite generously. He offered Serena a small house on the estate, plus an income for life of two thousand pounds a year, all of which she gratefully accepted, along with the conditions that went with it. These included finding and installing suitable tenants in the big house, to be accountable solely to her, and of undertaking to do whatever became necessary in the way of insurance, renovations and repairs for its proper maintenance. In short, she was to be agent, caretaker and glorified housekeeper rolled into one.

Pelham probably knew what he was doing too, for she was fanatically conscientious and probably earned her two thousand pounds and free house about four times over, for during all the years of her reign only the last two had brought her any peace of mind. Faced with a house which was too big for a single family and too eccentrically designed for a school or institution, the few remaining alternatives, which in this case had included a dubious health farm and a cranky religious order, had all turned out disastrously. It was only when James Kingley Farrer, known to his hundreds of intimates as Jake, arrived on the scene that things began to look up.

Jake, was well known to me by reputation as an elderly and celebrated Hollywood director, of Anglo-Irish origins, and his reason for coming to live in Herefordshire was not that it provided a peaceful seclusion for his retirement, but in order to embark on a whole new career. This was nothing less than to turn himself into an English country gentleman, with all the paraphernalia of guns and dogs, grooms and hunters, wine cellars and dinner parties, which in his romantic view the role required of him.

Chargrove Manor made an ideal launching pad for this enterprise, for Serena provided him with the few remaining assets which money could not buy and, in addition to her other duties, soon found herself arranging his parties, interviewing butlers, advising him where to buy his horses and introducing him to all her friends in the neighbourhood, none of which she resented in the slightest, and for three very good reasons.

The first was that she soon became sincerely attached to Jake, the second that he put her on the payroll under the heading of Hostess-Secretary, and the third and easily most compelling, that he appointed Primrose to manage and oversee the stables.

Primrose had just turned twenty when this change came about and was a heavy featured, sulky girl, too tall and powerfully built for her own comfort and depressingly devoid of charm. Aware, or fearful of her inability to compete with most of her contemporaries on their own terms, she had gone, in defiance, to the opposite extreme, dressing in the most hideous clothes she could find, gorging herself on starchy foods and truculently inviting everyone to give her animals, rather than people, any day of the week. To have the tiresome Primrose engaged in an occupation not only remunerative but so perfectly tailored to her temperament was the greatest blessing that anyone could have bestowed on Serena and the only tiny pill inside all this jam was the feeling of not playing quite fair to Pelham in accepting bounty from him and from his tenant simultaneously. She assured me that she had kept him informed, step by step, of these developments, but that she hardly knew whether he read her letters or not, since he never bothered to answer them.

The interesting prospect ahead was to discover what Pelham's reactions were, now that he had arrived and seen the situation at first hand.

CHAPTER THREE

1

ROBIN deposited me at West Lodge, which was the name of Serena's house, just after three o'clock, having turned down my suggestion that he and Sergeant Brook should step inside and revive themselves with a cup of tea. Unfortunately, Chargrove had proved to be even further out of his way than he had reckoned and still more time and temper had been lost by my inability to remember whether to turn left or right inside the main gates of the park and of having, as was inevitable in this tense situation, made the wrong guess.

The front door was ajar and I gave it a push with my suitcase and walked into the hall, making yoo-hooing noises to announce my arrival. No one answered, but I did not assume from this that it had passed unnoticed, for Nannie's room overlooked the drive and she kept an eye trained on everyone's comings and goings.

Dropping my case at the foot of the stairs, I walked on to the sitting room, which, having always been known as the parlour, was still known as the parlour. The name suited it too, for it was a snug and pretty place in its cluttered way, with several high, button-backed Victorian chairs, a spinet in one corner of the room and glass-fronted cupboards filled with Rockingham china in two of the others.

Serena was seated by the fireplace, with her nose stuck into the current piece of tapestry. It was a familiar sight, for this kind of fine needlework was both her favourite hobby and greatest accomplishment. In fact, considering the time she devoted to it, it was surprising that the end products did not adorn practically every piece of furniture in the house, but I suspected that she had cupboards full of finished canvases, hidden away and never used, having a fastidious prejudice against appearing to show off and suchlike vulgarity.

'Come along in, Tessa darling,' she said, sounding as delighted as the most demanding guest could wish. 'How lovely and punctual you are! And this is Lindy. Pelham's wife, you know. I've been telling her all about you.'

Lindy had been sitting on the hearthrug, with her knees drawn up to her chin, when I entered the room, but during Serena's introduction had sprung up and now offered me a tiny, childlike claw.

'Hi, Tessa!' she said, eyes ashine and in a voice redolent with warmth and insincerity.

I might have been less taken aback if they had told me I was to meet Pelham's new American grand-daughter, for by my reckoning he was now over fifty, whereas only the fact that Lindy was so busily acting the part of a seventeen-year-old prompted me to place her age as a year or two above that. She was a frail, doll-like creature, wearing an ankle length frilly cotton dress and no make-up. Her hair, which was long, blonde and straight, was pulled off her face and fastened in a tortoiseshell clip on the crown of her head and she had wide, innocent blue eyes. Once or thrice, as I got to know her better, I noticed a pensive look in the eyes and a slight hardening of the jaw, which did not quite fit the impulsive little bundle of friendliness she normally projected, but at first meeting the image was impressively adolescent.

'Sit down, both of you,' Serena said, folding away her work, 'and get to know each other while I make some tea. Or would you rather go upstairs, Tessa, after your long drive? I've put you in what we now call the apricot room. I do hope you won't mind?'

'No, I'm sure I won't,' I agreed, for it was a matter of profound indifference to me what they called it. 'But don't make tea specially for me. Shouldn't we wait for the others?'

'There's no need for that. Primrose isn't here. Jake has taken her over to Newmarket to look at a horse. They spent last night there and she won't be home until this evening; and Pelham's upstairs with Nannie. I expect she's giving him a real old nursery tea.'

'Listen!' Lindy said, bounding up from the floor again, 'why don't I make the tea? I know you two have lots to say to each other, and your kitchen's so darling, I'd just love to play around in it. Oh, do let me, Serena!'

I don't think she actually clapped her hands when permission was granted, but it was obviously a close thing.

'Sweet little creature,' Serena murmured absently when she had gone. 'So kind and helpful, I can't tell you!'

'The name suits her, I think.'

'Yes, doesn't it? You know, I asked her if it was short for Linda or Belinda or something like that, but she said no, her parents had christened her Lindy. They'd heard it in a song and thought it was a real name. Apparently, her family are farmers in Michigan or somewhere like that. Very good, high principled sort of people, but not much education, so she tells me. She made no secret of it. I rather admire that, don't you? I mean, not pretending to be something other than you are?'

'Yes, very much,' I replied. 'She's rather young for Pelham, isn't she?'

'In years perhaps, but Pelham's never really grown up. You'll see what I mean when you meet him. Still the same overgrown baby he always was. At least, that is . . . I suppose he has changed a bit in some ways.'

'Strange if he hadn't, surely? After all, it must be going on for twenty-five years since you saw him and he's spent the interval bumming round Canada and the States. How could he not have changed?'

'I don't think you could call it bumming around exactly. I gather he's recently been doing very well in what they call real estate.'

'Enough to change anyone! What's his purpose in coming here? Have you discovered yet?'

Serena had been jabbing her needle into the arm of her chair, pricking out little patterns with it, but now looked up at me and smiled:

'I'm so pleased you could come, Tessa. You have such a refreshingly down-to-earth attitude to things. It always acts like a tonic. And of course you're right. The truth is that I've carried a picture in my mind of Pelham all these years as a sort of older, slightly coarser version of Rupert as he used to be, but as you say, why should it be so, after the totally different sort of life he's led? And, if I were honest, I would have to admit that even Rupert might not have settled into exactly the mould I've invented for him. People have an awkward habit of developing along their own lines, don't they?'

This reflection evoked another memory and I asked:

'By the way, what in particular is Primrose sulking about just now?'

'Well, it's absurd really, but you know how childish she can be sometimes and the truth is she's madly jealous.'

'Of Pelham?'

'Yes. She resents his taking up so much of Nannie's time, for one thing, but the main trouble is this fixation about Pelham having stolen her birthright. It's all a lot of twaddle because, if the property hadn't passed to him, there's an uncle who would have inherited anyway. He's a clergy-man and pretty doddery now, so they tell me, but there's never been any question of breaking the entail, so long as a male heir exists. Besides, it's not Pelham's fault that things were arranged in that way, is it? You and I under-stand that perfectly well, but no one can get it through to Primrose and it does make the atmosphere rather tense.'

'Yes, it must, but presumably she'll accustom herself to the idea gradually; learn to accept him, I mean, now that he's become a reality, instead of some legendary figure living thousands of miles away.'

'Well, let's hope so, but you know how deep-rooted these obsessions are?'

'And I suppose, if Pelham has come over to inspect his property, with the idea of moving in eventually, it's going to make the problem even trickier?'

'Whatever is that child doing with our tea, I wonder?' Serena said, taking her attention away from me and tilt-ing her head towards the door. 'I'd better go and see what she's up to.'

Even as she spoke, some alarming crashes were heard from beyond the door and, in passing by me to open it, Serena laid a hand on my shoulder in what I took to be a restraining gesture, although I could see no reason for it.

Lindy had found an enormous black tin tray, which I felt sure had never found its way outside the kitchen before in its whole career, had covered it with paper tissues and piled on a vast selection of unmatching crockery. She set it down on the sofa table and then stood back and beamed at us both triumphantly:

'How's that for a first attempt at tea making?' she asked in breathless wonder. 'Look, I found cookies . . . and jam . . . and . . . and honey!' she went on excitedly, as though confident that Serena would be bowled over to learn that she possessed these items in her larder.

'Very clever, darling! Tessa and I were just saying what a luxury it is to sit here gossiping while someone else does all the work. Now, are you going to pour out for us too?'

So, evidently, for all her admiring protestations, Serena was not yet ready to include Lindy in any family discussion. I did not in the least regret the ban, in so far as it related to Primrose, for there had already been indications that I should be obliged to hear a good deal more on this subject during the forthcoming weekend. I was more curious, and at the same time less confident about tracking down the reasons for Serena's untypical evasiveness on the question of Pelham.

One compensation was that I had not long to wait to form my own impressions of him, for at this point he arrived in person, swaggering into the room, placing his open palm against the back of Lindy's neck, before twisting her head round to give her a smacking kiss.

This ceremony concluded, he took the cup of tea which she had been in the act of handing to Serena, walked with it to the fireplace where I was standing, embraced me warmly and said in the laziest of drawls:

'Hallo, my darling! You must be the famous little god-daughter! Lovely to see you again!'

I daresay that most people who spend long periods abroad end by falling into one of two categories. They either work overtime at acquiring local colour, becoming more papal than the pope, or else cling with such tenacity to their native characteristics that they end up as caricatures of the original. Perhaps for Englishmen the second course is more usual and Pelham had certainly followed it. His accent, clothes, even his haircut so typified a certain type of outdated stage aristocrat that I half expected him to suggest that we all went to Monte Carlo.

Another surprise was that he did not look at all as I had pictured him. It was true that he was tall and dark and bold looking, with a somewhat arrogant manner, which was just as I had expected, but after that reality and imagination parted company. The mistake of course had been the same as Serena's, of assuming that he would be a replica of an older Rupert, minus the black eye patch. I had no personal recollection whatever of Rupert, but the house was crammed with photographs of him at every stage of his short life, beginning with the beady eyed baby sitting up in its pram and glaring at the photographer, which adorned Nannie's mantelpiece, right up to the snapshots of the aloof aquiline young man which had been taken only weeks before his death.

There was nothing remotely aquiline about Pelham, for he was stout and flabby, with a loose, pouting lower lip, and age had coarsened his features as well. Sensual rather than aloof was the word to describe him, and never more so than when his eyes turned towards his wife.

'Oh, come now, Pelham,' Serena was saying in her mildly reproving tone, 'you can't seriously pretend to remember Tessa. She was only a tiny little girl when she came down to stay with my parents.'

'Oh yes, I do,' he insisted, putting an arm round my shoulder. 'I remember her perfectly. It was just before I sailed away, and what's more I remember how my naughty brother scared the wits out of her by wrapping himself in a tiger skin rug and yowling at the poor pet, so that she never stopped screaming for the rest of the afternoon. Unbelievable, it was.'

'Oh yes,' Lindy chirruped, 'I remember you told me about that, Pel. Wasn't that an awful thing to do? My goodness, Tessa, I can't imagine why you don't have phobias about it to this day.'

'I don't know,' Serena said unhappily. 'Nannie has told me that story too, several times; but somehow it still doesn't seem real to me. I suppose the truth is, I've tried to remember only the good things about Rupert.'

There was a brief, uncomfortable silence, which she broke by saying quickly:

'Well, come along, Tessa darling. If you've finished your tea, let's go upstairs and make sure you've got everything you need.'

2

'You mustn't forget to go next door and say hallo to Nannie,' she reminded me when we reached my bedroom. It was a tiny, east facing room on the top floor in what had originally been the attics and then become part of the nursery suite when Serena moved in. Primrose and Nannie still occupied the old day and night nurseries and I believe the apricot room had functioned as a combined box room and pantry. However, Serena had unexceptional taste, of a highly conventional style, and this, combined with her new affluence had transformed it into a positive bower of blossomed wallpaper and apricot velvet curtains.

'No, I won't,' I assured her. 'How is the old . . . battleaxe?'

'Failing a little, I think. She had a lot of pain in her shoulder about a month ago and, although no one realised it at the time, it seems that it could have been a mild coronary. Then there's the perennial indigestion, which she plagues us all with, although it's simply because she will overeat.'

'Honestly, Serena, you never cease to amaze me! Who else but you would keep an old family retainer on the premises in this day and age? Didn't you know that sort of thing went out years ago?'

'Yes, lots of people have told me so, but heaven knows how they dispose of them when they get old and feeble and have been with the family for nearly half a century. Nan's over eighty now, you know.'

'And likely to live to a hundred and four, the way you cosset her. Couldn't she go to some old people's home, where they'd keep her in order a bit? Somewhere nearby, where you and Primrose could visit her?'

'My dear child, how could I be so heartless, when I have room enough here? She stood by me, you know, when I had no one else to turn to, and this is her home, just as much as mine. Besides, Rupert would . . .'

'Turn in his grave?'

She laughed: 'I believe I was going to say something absurd like that, though of course it makes even less sense when someone is cremated. All the same, I do understand what people mean by the expression. If Rupert had known he was going to die, I feel sure he would have made some proper provision for her, and for Primrose and me as well, but how could he have known? He was twenty-six years old and they told him he had appendicitis. Still, wherever his spirit is now, I am sure it would give me no peace if I were to put his old Nan into a home.'

'That's all very well, but it's not his spirit which has to live with her.'

'No, although he would be much more patient with her than I am. And Pelham's the same; he's been an absolute brick in that way, spends practically every minute of the day with her, talking over old times, which of course is the one thing she really enjoys and can't get enough of. I'm afraid I'm very inadequate in that respect. She tells me these stories over and over again about things that happened when the boys were little and half the time she gets the dates mixed up and confuses Rupert with Primrose, and I must confess that I find this continual dwelling on the past rather a bore.'

'Me too. I'd go raving mad if I had to spend every day with her.'

'Primrose doesn't mind a bit, though; she positively enjoys it. It must be a family characteristic, I suppose, but Pelham really has surprised me. I certainly didn't expect to find him so wrapped up in the past, specially now he has this new young wife he's so obviously mad about. Wasn't it strange, his getting married at his age?'

'Perhaps he decided it was time he had an heir?'

'No, apparently she can't ever have children. I'm not sure why, but they both knew all about it when they married.'

'Just as well, from your point of view, I suppose; but doesn't she resent his spending so much time up in the nursery? All this old history can't be much of a thrill for her?'

'Well, she doesn't have to listen to it herself, of course, but funnily enough she positively encourages Pelham. Most young women of her age might be rather irritated by it, but she's so very sweet and understanding.'

'Do you know how long they mean to stay?' I asked, 'or why they've come at all? I assume it wasn't purely on Nannie's account?'

Serena had been fussing round the room while we talked, turning down the bed and touching up the flowers and evidently her mind had now switched back to an earlier topic, for she sat down on the dressing table stool, regarding me with great seriousness as she said:

'And, you know, Tessa, it's not really up to me to make the decisions about Nannie. I may find her a bore and a mischief maker, but as I've said, that's not Primrose's view at all. She's absolutely devoted to Nan and would never, never consent to my sending her away.'

'Then the best thing would be for Primrose to marry and have Nannie to live with her.'

'I used to think that might be the solution in the end,' Serena admitted, 'but there doesn't seem to be much prospect of it at present. She won't even look at young men. At one time it looked as though she and Richard Soames might hit it off. He's the young doctor who took over my father's practice, if you remember? But somehow it all fizzled out. I am afraid Nannie may have put it into her head that he wasn't good enough for her, which is arrant nonsense of course, but she's stuffed the child's head with so many fairy tales about her wonderful, glamorous father and uncle that all the boys she meets in real life seem terribly weedy and dim by comparison. It worries me really, because it's not as though she had a career to support herself on. She's dabbled about with all sorts of ideas, like training to be a vet and going to an agricultural college, but the trouble was that I could never afford much in the way of an education for her and you'd be surprised how many qualifications you need nowadays even to look after animals. That's why I was so delighted when this job with Jake came along. I thought at least it would get her out of the house and make her learn to stand on her own feet, but I'm not so sure now that it was the right thing to do.'

'Why not?'

'Because it has thrown her right into the very surroundings which all her fantasies are built on and it's still more fuel to the flames. Not only is she spending her days in the house which she sees as rightfully hers, but it's also the scene of all those dashing and romantic exploits she's been fed on since she was a baby. If I'd had any sense, I'd have realised that substituting the big house for the nursery was the very last thing to cure her of these delusions. In fact, all it has done is to harden them.'

'Cheer up!' I said. 'Perhaps the cure will come all by itself, without any effort on your part. I mean, now that she's actually met Pelham, the truth will soon sink in that he's not a knight in shining armour, but just an ordinary middle-aged uncle, and the stardust is bound to fall from her eyes, don't you think? Well, no, I suppose that's ridiculous, really.'

'Why do you say so? I thought you'd made a very good point.'

'But, you see, Serena, after making it, it struck me that, middle-aged uncle or not, he can hardly be all that ordinary if he's snared someone so young and pretty as Lindy. You and I may not be exactly bowled over, but he probably has some irresistible attraction for the romantic teenager.'

'Oh no, I don't agree with that at all. Fundamentally, he's not in the least the type that Primrose admires. I think you were right the first time and that she'll soon be thoroughly disillusioned. Or rather, she'll get the whole thing into perspective. Well, bless you for coming, dearest. It's such a relief to pour my petty little problems into a sympathetic ear. And now I must go and battle with the really serious problem of dinner. Alice Thorne is very kindly coming in to give me a hand with it, but don't breathe a word of that to Nannie or she'll send her tray down untouched and we shall have more trouble on our hands.'

Since the reasons for my invitation to West Lodge had been made abundantly clear, I could scarcely complain if the choice of topics for discussion were Serena's rather than mine, but it had not escaped me that both my attempts to delve any deeper into the motives and plans of the returning prodigal had been blandly evaded. So, having drawn a blank with her, I found a new approach to the subject and invited Lindy to come for a walk in the park before the sun went down.

CHAPTER FOUR

1

CHARGROVE House was only ten minutes walk from West Lodge by way of its formal approach, a continuation of the main drive, but halfway along it Lindy and I struck off to the right, following a footpath which meandered round to a walled kitchen garden behind the stable block.

The drive was bordered, on either side, by a sloping grass verge, backed by tall trees and with flowering shrubs and smaller ornamental trees in the foreground. Some of the trees must have been planted centuries before, and doubtless there had been a house on the present site for even longer than that, but the existing residence was the work of the shipping grandfather, who had much to answer for, as it was an ill-proportioned, red brick Edwardian pile, heavily overloaded with gables and somewhat resembling a blown up, rustic labour exchange. It was not nearly so spacious as it appeared from outside, consisting of a relatively small number of poky rooms linked together by a series of immensely long and draughty corridors, but the exterior was quite awe-inspiring in its size and vulgarity.

'How does it feel to be the owner of all this?' I asked Lindy, with a sweeping gesture of the hand to indicate that I referred to the setting rather than the house. 'Pretty good, I imagine?'

'I don't feel in the least like any of it does belong to me.'

'No? Still, it's amazing how one can adapt oneself to new ideas. I daresay this one will grow on you.'

'No, honestly, Tessa, I think it'll more likely just fade away like a dream, or like something I read about in a book, but never really experienced.'

'But when you're actually living here . . .'

'Living here?' she squealed. 'Whatever gave you the idea we intended living here?'

'I suppose I just took it for granted. I know it couldn't happen immediately, but I believe Jake only has it on a short lease and it is Pelham's house, after all. It would be natural for him to want to retire here in his old age.'

'Gosh, no, Tessa, please believe me, you've got it all wrong. This just happens to be a stopover on our world trip. Soon as it's over, we'll be back where we started out from, in good old California. Naturally, when we were planning it we wanted to take in England and meet some of Pelham's folks and I'm so happy we did. I think Serena's just adorable, though she scares me some.'

'So how long do you mean to stay?'

'Two, three weeks, I guess. We're going to Paris after this and then home. Goodness, I can't wait to see Paris. I bet you've been there lots of times, haven't you? You know something, Tessa?'

'What?'

'This is the very first time in my whole life I've been abroad.'

'And now you have, aren't you tempted to stay?'

'Oh, I want to see every bit of it I can while I'm here, but it's not for me, that I do know. Please don't misunderstand me though, Tessa. I think this country is beautiful, I really do. I never saw anywhere so green, green, green; but it's not for me, period.'

'And yet you were brought up in the country, weren't you? Serena tells me your family had a farm.'

'Sure they did and could I wait to get away from it? The short answer is No. My father was okay, my mother I hated.'

'Where are they now?'

'My mother's still there, with her churchgoing and her sewing circle. My father died a year or two back. Guess I've been searching for someone to take his place ever since. What they call an oedipus in reverse.'

'You don't say!'

'Anyway, where we lived wasn't anything like this. I couldn't have imagined a place like this even existed.'

'Didn't Pelham tell you about it?'

We were sitting on a fallen tree trunk, resting from the uphill climb and she leant over sideways, so that her hair fell forward, hiding her face, and plucked a blade of grass which she began to chew. After a few nibbles she said:

'Yes, in a way, he did, but it was more like things that happened here than the place itself. Probably he just took that for granted.'

'How did you and Pelham meet, by the way?'

'Through my room mate, Else. I was in school in Southern California; college, I guess you'd call it. I majored in biology. Else's parents had this place out at Santa Barbara. She and I were vacationing out there one weekend and Pelham came for dinner. He was a business colleague of Else's father. Soon as I graduated we got married. The story of my life.'

'Well, it's only just begun,' I reminded her, 'and, further-more you may change your mind about coming to live here when you get to know it better. Sometimes the English countryside gets a grip on people after a while. Look at old Jake.'

'His age, you can understand it,' she said, throwing away the mangled blade of grass with a somewhat symbolic gesture. 'Me, I've still got places to go, things to do. You know?'

'Come with me,' I said. 'Let me take you by the hand and I'll show you something to make you change your mind.'

I stood up and, following the path a little further, led her through the green door into the walled kitchen garden. The late afternoon sun had turned the bricks to a rosy pink and the ripening pears to a golden yellow. Every conceivable variety of fruit and vegetable seemed to be flourishing in this mellow and peaceful enclosure, each in its own straight, pristine row. The tomatoes were warm to the touch and the scent of lavender and sweet peas, bordering the gravel walks hung on the air. The only sound was the hum of bees and there was even an eighteenth-century yokel type bent double among the gooseberry bushes, in breeches and a round felt hat, to add to the timeless quality. It was a scene to awaken the acquisitive spirit in anyone and I said:

'I think I'd even put up with that monstrosity of a house, if they'd throw this in.'

'Sure! Dig it up and make a pool. Who eats all this stuff, anyway?'

'Funnily enough, I never thought of that. I have no idea.'

'Well, I'm just a lousy Philistine, you see. No soul.'

'I must ask Serena, or Pelham perhaps. No, on second thoughts, we'd better not remind Pelham about this particular corner of his property. I am sure it must be full of nostalgic memories and it might start tugging at the heartstrings.'

Lindy shook her head: 'Uh uh. He's immune now. Honestly, Tessa, please believe me, if he really felt he belonged here I wouldn't stand in his way, but he doesn't. It all happened too long ago and he's made a new life now.'

'Then we'll ask him what happens to all his produce. I'd really be fascinated to know.'

'Most of it is sold, as a matter of fact,' the yokel figure said, emerging from the gooseberry bushes and revealing itself to be Primrose. 'Jake has first pickings and Mum takes what she needs, when she remembers to ask for it. The outdoor staff get their whack and the rest goes to market twice a week. Satisfied?'

'More than. I thought you were in Newmarket?'

'I was. Went over to look at a five-year-old Jake's trainer brought back from Ireland. Got back about an hour ago. I thought Mum might be able to use a few gooseberries, as she's got such a houseful. Jake can't touch 'em. They don't go with his diabetes.'

Her face was brick red and dampish, under the dirty old felt hat, her hands swollen and scratched and her manner as abrasive as ever. She looked even clumsier and more ungainly than usual beside the elf-like Lindy and yet, so far from manifesting the usual symptoms of inferiority, there was a confidence, even a hint of suppressed excitement about her. Her right thumb had started to bleed and she kept sucking it, with an air of secretive relish, as though actually enjoying the exercise.

'You going back to the Lodge now?' she enquired, giving the thumb a rest. 'If so, you can take these, if you like. Save me a journey.'

'Okay. How about you, though? Won't you be home this evening?'

'Oh, I've masses of jobs to get through before I can knock off. Just scrape home in time for dinner, if I'm lucky. Tell Mum not to wait for me.'

Lindy went straight upstairs, colliding on the half landing with Pelham, who came bounding down from the floor above. He clasped her round the waist, swung her into the air and then stood watching, with a complacent smile on his face, as she tripped away.

'Oh, yum yum, lovely goosegogs!' he said, having torn his eyes away from this vision and joined me in the hall. 'Are they for my dins?'

'Could be, if anyone has time to top and tail. Do you like them?'

'Adore them,' he said, picking up a handful of the shiny green berries and letting them fall through his fingers, 'worship the ground they grow on. Goosegogs! Isn't that a marvellous word? Nan's just been bullying me all over again about the times when I used to escape from her clutches and hide out in the kitchen garden, making an absolute pig of myself. What happened to the kitchen garden, by the way? I hope that fellow, Jake, hasn't dug it up and made a swimming pool?'

'No, it's still there.'

'And just the same?'

'Exactly the same.'

'What bliss! Lovely to know that a few things don't change, isn't it, my pretty one?' he asked, pausing only to ruffle my hair before galloping out of the house, as though intent on verifying the matter for himself with the least possible delay.

I walked on to the kitchen, wondering whether it was he or his wife who had mis-read the script.

'Didn't Mrs Thorne turn up, after all?' I asked, placing the basket on the deal topped table. Serena was at the other end of it, rolling out pastry on a marble slab.

'Indeed she did, and she's laying the table for me, which is a job I hate. I must say, it's marvellous to have her back. She's not the world's most inspired cook, but wonderfully thorough and conscientious and she'll turn her hand to anything. I have great hopes of Alice; Mrs Thorne, rather. I really must try to remember not to call her Alice. For some reason she feels it's demeaning, so do remember too, won't you? The last thing we want is to upset her.'

'She used to work for you before, didn't she?'

'Yes, before she lost her little boy.'

'Which must be what? Ten or twelve years ago?'

'More than that. Primrose was only six at the time, which is why we thought we could hide it from her. We told her that Alan had gone to visit his grandmother in Scotland. Great mistake, of course. You can't conceal things in a close little community like this, where everyone knows everyone else's business. Primrose soon got hold of the truth, or part of it, which was even worse. I think if we'd explained it to her tactfully it wouldn't have been half so bad in the end. It was piecing together the bits of gossip and filling in the gaps with her own imagination which did the real harm. She used to get the most terrible nightmares and it was months before she could be persuaded to go anywhere near that side of the park.'

'Has Mrs Thorne got over it now?'

'No, I don't think one ever would, do you? Alan was her only child and they never had any more. She was half insane, poor dear, for a year or two, but of course she's got through that stage now. All the same, I don't believe such scars could ever heal completely. She may not suffer any more, but that's only because she's numbed. This must sound callous, Tess, but it's one reason why, apart from being so hardworking and efficient, I feel she could be such a boon to me.'

'I don't know whether it's callous or not, but it's certainly mystifying.'

'Well, you see, even when Nan does find out that Alice, Mrs Thorne, I mean, is working here again, I don't think she'll find it so easy to spoil things. You can't touch nerves on the raw when they've already been blunted.'

'You think she'll have a damn good try, though?'

'Yes, I'm afraid so. She's so dreadfully jealous and possessive, you see. It almost amounts to a disease; and unfortunately she's particularly set against anyone who comes to work here. I tried several different women after Alice left me, but not one of them was able to stick it for more than a few months.'

'But surely, Serena, if you explained that she's senile, they'd understand and just ignore her?'

'The trouble is that she's very clever at finding out people's sensitive spots and jabbing away at them; and I suppose I was weak minded and let her get away with things in the beginning, instead of putting my foot down. It didn't matter so much, you see, in the early days, when she could pull her weight and do all the washing and ironing and so on, but she's long past that now. In fact, it's the other way round and she's the one who makes most work of all. Now that I can afford it at last, it would be nice at my age to have some regular help. This is not a big house, as you know, but we're a long way from the shops and there's an awful lot to do, with three of us living here all the time. Sometimes I feel quite worn out.'

'I can imagine and I think it's far too much for you to cope with on your own. Let's hope that Mrs Thorne provides the answer.'

'I pray she will too, and the signs are quite promising. She's been doing little errands for me and odd jobs at home, ever since Pelham and Lindy turned up, and she's promised to come and lend a hand over the weekend, so one must just carry on from day to day and hope for the best. Ah, there you are, Mrs Thorne dear!' she added, raising her voice and enunciating more clearly, 'and I was just saying how nice it was to have you back with us again. You remember Mrs Price, don't you? Miss Tessa as was?'

She was a straight backed, bloodless looking woman, probably no older than Serena, but looking at least sixty, with thin lips and a forbidding expression. However, she smiled and shook my hand, saying that indeed she did remember and that it was a funny thing but someone had mentioned seeing me in a film only the other day. Then, as though grasping every opportunity to be amiable, she began to praise the gooseberries.

'Not that I can touch them myself,' she added, in the tone of one with whom looking on the dark side had become a habit, 'too acid for me.'

'These are beauties, though, aren't they?' Serena said. 'If you get time you might put them in the tart, instead of the apples. Did you pick all that lot yourself, Tessa?'

'No, Primrose did and she asked me to deliver them. She's back, by the way. I forgot to tell you. She's back and she hopes to scrape home in time for dinner. Her own words.'

'Oh dear, that sounds ominous! I do hope she'll be back in time to change. It rather puts people off their food to have her sitting there smelling of the stables, and I'm sure Pelham hates that sort of thing. Which reminds me, it's time I went and had a bath myself. I'm sure Mrs Thorne has made the table look so nice, and we mustn't let her down. Use my bathroom when I'm out, will you, Tessa? That will leave the nursery one free for Primrose, so at least she won't have that excuse.'

'Would you like me to top and tail these for you, while I'm waiting?' I asked, when Serena had gone.

'No, don't you bother, Miss. I'm in plenty of time.'

She was walking away from me as she spoke, making for the larder, a vast stone floored cave leading off the kitchen, which had started life as a dairy. However, something in her tone gave me the impression that I had not yet been dismissed and, sure enough, when she emerged a few seconds later, bearing a handsome looking joint of beef on a white dish, she said:

'I was wondering what you thought about this? It's some time since I cooked one this size and I want to get it just right for her, if I can. How long would you leave it in, if it was you?'

'Well, I'm no expert, I have to tell you. I usually stick to the formula of fifteen minutes per pound and fifteen extra for the pot.'

'Yes, that's my method, as a rule, but they're tricky things, these sirloins, and there's all this bone to be taken into account,' she said, prodding it with her finger. 'It must have cost her a pretty penny and I wouldn't like it to get spoilt in the cooking.'

'Oh, don't worry, I'm sure you'll manage it perfectly, and there's one thing I can tell you.'

'What's that?'

'If anything should go wrong, Mrs Hargrave would never dream of blaming you for it.'

'I know that,' she said. 'No one better. I've never had so much as a sharp word in all the years I've known her, and she was goodness itself to me when I had my trouble. There's not a mortal thing I wouldn't do for her, if it lay in my power.'

She was regarding me so earnestly and speaking with such great intensity that I wondered if, perhaps too shy and inarticulate to express these sentiments openly, she was depending on me to pass them on. One thing I became convinced of, as I climbed the stairs to my little apricot box, was that in describing Mrs Thorne as a woman now drained of emotion and with all passion spent, Serena had made a grave error of judgement, and one which did not bode well for future domestic harmony.

With this thought in mind, and considering it to be as good a moment as any to pay my duty call, I did not go directly to my room, but stopped outside the nursery door and, having knocked and identified myself, obeyed the command to step inside.

CHAPTER FIVE

1

IT WAS like straying on to a set for a family comedy of the thirties. The Peter Pan motif of the wallpaper was repeated in the shade on the ceiling lamp above the circular table, which was covered by a red woollen cloth and had a jam jar crammed with wild flowers standing near the edge of it. The cork floor was painted blue and scattered with faded nursery rhyme rugs, and there were Christmas annuals and school stories between book ends on top of the low white cupboard and, beside them, a vast collection of bottles and tins, including prickly heat powder, milk of magnesia and syrup of figs, among other kindred delights. There was even an old-fashioned portable gramophone, and only the absence of a cot and of tiny garments airing on the iron guard round the Victorian fireplace indicated that the room was no longer inhabited by a child.

Seated in her cane rocking chair beside the fireplace, Nannie looked as though she were waiting for the next replacement to arrive, her ample lap making do with a bundle of dark green knitting during the enforced delay.

She was a Buddha-like figure, immensely stout and with malevolent, boot button eyes, and she wore a white bibbed apron over a grey overall, grey stockings and fur trimmed bedroom slippers.

'How are you, Nannie? Looking fine, I see,' I said, in the somewhat sycophantic tone I invariably found myself adopting in her presence.

'You've taken your time,' she said, glaring at me accusingly. 'Mummie told me you got here just before three.'

'Well, you see, I had tea and then I went for a walk and then I came straight here.'

'Well, come in and shut the door, there's a good girl. These draughts are no good for my rheumatism.'

I had been hoping to limit my visit to a few minutes' hover round the open door, but there was no withstanding the voice which had moulded and scolded two generations and I obeyed, seating myself on the chair opposite her.

'And how does it feel to have Pelham back? Has he changed much?'

'Be funny if he hadn't, wouldn't it?' she snapped, throwing my own words back at me, and then adding more thoughtfully:

'No, if I speak the truth, he hasn't changed all that much. Not in his ways, that is. Still the same young scamp as he always was, bless him! Have you met that wife of his?'

'Yes, rather sweet, don't you think?'

'Not what I'd call sweet, and not the one I'd have chosen for my boy. I can't stand these yankee voices and goodness knows where she was dragged up, nosey parkering her way into everything. Didn't much fancy what she saw, by the looks of it. Real little fidgety Phil. Pelham brought her up to be introduced to his poor old Nan, but she's never bothered to come back since.'

'She's shy, I expect. Pretty, though; you must admit that.'

'Couldn't say. These poor old eyes of mine don't see much these days. Sitting where you are, you're nothing but a blur to me, did you know that?'

'No, but it doesn't particularly surprise me. Most of the time I'm nothing but a blur to myself.'

'So sharp you'll cut yourself one of these fine days, I shouldn't wonder. Oh, I can see to do this knitting all right,' she went on, answering the unspoken question. 'Made so many in my time, I could do them in my sleep. I'd like to know what's become of my glasses though. Some fool of a woman Mummie got in to do the cleaning must have broken them and didn't dare own up, very likely. Not that it matters, I suppose. I know where to put my hand on everything in this little room and these poor old legs are too full of rheumatism nowadays to move far outside it. As for my indigestion, well, you'd really pity me if I was to tell you about it.'

'What is it you're making?' I asked, reluctant to be put to the test.

'This? Oh, it's another jersey for Rupert; Primrose, I should say. Don't think much of the colour, do you? I prefer the pastel shades myself, but she says it's got to be something that doesn't show the dirt.'

'I think she's right. What I mean is, pastel shades are rather Out at the moment.'

'Oh, are they? Well, you'd know, I suppose, gallivanting about like you do. Here, hold this up against yourself and see how it looks. You'll swim in it, we know that, but you're something of the same colouring as my great elephant of a girl.'

'What do you think?' I mumbled, gripping the needles with my chin.

'Not bad. You are a skinny morsel though, aren't you? There's a long glass in the night nursery, if you want to have a proper look.'

When I returned she was heaving with silent mirth and wiping her eyes on the hem of her apron.

'I couldn't help laughing,' she explained, taking charge of the knitting again. 'It put me in mind of the time when one of the aunts, Mrs Jameson I suppose it must have been, took Rupert and Primrose up to Harrods – Oh, there I go again! Rupert and Pelham is what I should have said . . . up to Harrods to get them some new jerseys. You'll see the funny side of this, you having such a sense of humour. About eight years old they must have been at the time, and proper little monkeys, I don't mind telling you . . .'

The extraordinary thing about Nannie was that, despite her villainy, she had distinct charm when she chose to exert it and her stories, however rambling and highly coloured, could sometimes be hilarious. I could not imagine why she should put herself out for me in this way, or of what use I could be to her as an ally, if that indeed was her purpose, but when Serena put her head round the door to announce that the bathroom was free, I was staggered to find that I had been sitting in the nursery for all of half an hour and had not been bored in the least.

'Make yourself look nice and come down as soon as you're dressed,' Serena instructed me when I joined her on the landing. 'I've had a brilliant idea.'

'Aren't you going to tell me what it is?' I asked, as she started down the stairs.

'No, can't stop now, I must confer with Mrs Thorne; but remember what I said. It will be all hands to the pump this evening.'

2

Spurred on by this rallying call, I endeavoured to strike the delicate balance between making myself look nice and not taking too long about it and, sprinting out of the bathroom some twenty minutes later, was halted in my tracks on reaching the upper landing by the ominous and familiar sound of Nannie's voice raised in anger. The next minute Mrs Thorne stumbled out of the nursery and almost knocked me over as, with head bent, she plunged towards the stairs.

'Oh, beg pardon,' she mumbled, flattening herself against the wall to let me pass. There was nothing amiable in her manner now. She was red in the face and, although her lip trembled and her eyes were clouded by tears, these were all too obviously the manifestations of rage or mortification.

'What's up?' I asked. 'Has that old woman been making trouble again?'

'She's no business to say such things to me,' Mrs Thorne muttered. 'She's wicked, that's what she is, downright wicked! As though I hadn't put up with enough, without being accused of . . .' She pressed a hand to her mouth, as though to stop the flow of words, and I said:

'Forgive my asking, but didn't Mrs Hargrave warn you that she was liable to make a scene if she discovered you were here and that it might be advisable to keep out of her way?'

'Yes, but just now she asked me to bring the water carafes up to the bedrooms and I thought I might as well go and say good evening to Nannie, to sort of break the ice. Between you and me, I thought it was silly trying to pretend I wasn't here, because you can't keep anything secret from her for two minutes, and I've got nothing to be ashamed of, have I? I can work where I please, without her permission. Besides, I'd found her glasses, you see. At least, I guessed they were hers and that gave me a good opportunity.'

'Where did you find them?'

'In the spare room, where Mr Pelham's sleeping. Goodness knows how they got there, but I daresay she was poking about one day, when someone was staying here, and then she forgot where she'd left them.'

'Whereabouts in the spare room?'

'In that silver biscuit barrel thing. I was just taking a look to make sure the biscuits hadn't gone stale, because I remembered from the old days that they used to be left there for months on end, without anyone touching them, and there they were; her glasses, I mean. Whoever it was who was staying must have found them and popped them in for safe keeping. I thought she'd be ever so pleased and it would sort of clear the air, but not a bit of it. You'd have thought I'd done it purposely to aggravate, and you should have heard the dreadful, cruel things she said to me. Guilty conscience, I shouldn't wonder. Didn't like me knowing what she'd been up to.'

'Yes, I expect that's all it was.'

'Well, I wouldn't have given her away, if only she'd been a bit civil about it, but she needn't worry. I shan't be doing her any more good turns in a hurry. She's seen the last of me. Well, this won't get the parsnips buttered, will it? I must go down and get on with dinner.'

'Mrs Thorne!' I called softly, but she was halfway downstairs and did not hear me. Unwilling to risk being overheard in the nursery, I went after her, still calling her name:

'Mrs Thorne, listen a minute! I do hope that what you said just now – I do hope it doesn't mean you won't be coming here any more, because . . . you know . . .'

'No, don't worry yourself on that account, Miss. I shan't be leaving. It's what she wants, after all, isn't it? And I wouldn't give her the satisfaction. No, that's not at all my way of getting even with her.'

CHAPTER SIX

1

SERENA was alone in the parlour, every inch the gracious hostess, with needle poised over the tapestry and wearing a long, pale blue silk dress, which perfectly suited her alabaster complexion.

'Yes, isn't it gorgeous to sit back and be a lady, for once?' she asked when I had complimented her on this turn out. 'It's not the cooking I mind, you know; in fact, I quite enjoy that part. It's the dishing up which defeats me. I can never understand how some women manage it so smoothly, without getting crimson in the face and spattered with gravy. What kept you so long, my dearest? I thought you were never coming.'

'I ran into a little fraças upstairs. Nothing important. I'll tell you about it some time, but the great news is that Primrose is back. Splashing about in the bath too, to judge by noises off.'

'I know, you can hear every sound from that bathroom, can't you? I wish now that we'd put it between the other two rooms, instead of next to yours, but one can never foresee how things are going to turn out, can one? And it's marvellous about Primrose. All thanks to my little ruse, I might tell you.'

'That's right, you were going to elucidate.'

'Well, darling I'm sure you'll say I'm vain and silly, because people always ought to be admired for their own qualities, and not for what others try to make them out to be, but you see I'm afraid Primrose made rather a poor impression on Pelham when they first met. Once he gets to know her properly, of course, he'll soon realise how fundamentally good she is, but it would be so unfortunate if he were to be put off before there's been a chance for that.'

'Well, yes, Serena, I can understand your maternal pride not wanting to take a knock and all that, but does it really make so much difference what they think of each other? Pelham will be going back to London on Monday and Lindy assures me that they're moving on to Paris soon afterwards, so I can't see that it's of any great moment.'

'It is to me,' Serena answered. 'He's head of the family, after all, and she ought to have her proper place in it. She may never marry and I should hate to think of her being written off as a poor relation, of no account to anyone. Also I'm sure she has always suffered acutely from growing up without a father, from actually being born without one. I suppose if I'd been unselfish I'd have married again and provided a substitute, but I've never been able to contemplate sharing my life with anyone but Rupert. It would be a weight off my mind if Pelham could deputise for him to some extent with Primrose.'

'Right,' I agreed, 'so that's the battleground, and now tell me about the strategy. What threats and torture did you use to get the campaign off to such a flying start?'

'I had the brilliant idea of inviting Jake to dine here tonight.'

'Oh!' I said, somewhat deflated by this tame explanation. 'Did you really? And what's so miraculous about that?'

'Well, can't you see? It's all so beautifully neat, really. If Jake had been dining on his own, he'd have kept Primrose there until the last possible moment, chatting about withers and girths and all the rest of it for hours on end, anything to delay the terrors of solitude. He'd never admit it, but he's really very lonely, you know, in these alien surroundings, but also very meticulous and conventional, and once he'd been invited here, he'd be conscious of the need for both of them to smarten themselves up. So he'd make sure she got home early for once, which is exactly what has happened. It was a pity that by the time I'd thought of it Mrs Thorne had already made the gooseberry tart because, being diabetic, he can't eat them, but she's going to knock up some caramel custard as well, so he'll never know he was invited as an afterthought.'

'Clever thinking!' I said. 'And congratulations! But tell me one thing: won't the advantages of Primrose wafting around and smelling of Lifebuoy be outweighed by having Jake as a fellow guest? You said he was such a bore.'

'Well, a little heavy on hand, I admit and, like most people who have nothing to say, rather inclined to say it twice over, but Pelham must be quite accustomed to that, and no one could be kinder and more generous than Jake. We're all devoted to him.'

The deep sincerity with which this praise was uttered caused a strange and beautiful notion to take possession of me, whereby the relationship between her and Jake, so solidly founded as it was on mutual trust and economic convenience, might blossom into an even more romantic flower and that, with a little help from her god-daughter and other well disposed parties, she would yet return as mistress of Chargrove. It was but a step from there to the next move in the game, that of prevailing on Lindy, who, on her own and everyone else's admission was in the strongest position to do so, to persuade Pelham to grant his tenant a permanent lease. However, on the principle of clearing away unwanted debris first, I asked Serena if Jake had a wife.

'I believe not. There have been several, as you might expect, but I understand the last one died in rather tragic circumstances only a year or two ago.'

'What tragic circumstances?'

'I forget the details, but I gather she took an overdose or something. He's never referred to it, though and naturally I wouldn't dream of asking.'

So far so good, but I could not glean any more information for the time being, because we were joined by Pelham and Lindy, the latter wearing a pink and silver sari. She told me, when I reeled about in admiration, that she'd bought it in the bazaar in India, but had been so frightened of all those terribly starving people spitting and crowding in on her that she'd never nerved herself to take it out of its wrappings until this evening. She did not reveal where she had acquired her new found confidence.

Primrose arrived next, looking oddly distinguished in a long black skirt and purple, hand knitted pullover. By no stretch of the most charitable imagination could she have been called good looking, but at least she had combed her hair and dabbed on a bit of lipstick. The secret look of satisfaction was still much in evidence.

Jake came last of all, a tall, rangy man with a leonine head and deeply grooved lines in his face. It was interesting to discover that he had chosen the opposite extreme from Pelham's and taken on all the more flamboyant features of his adopted fellow countrymen. Besides looking like a superannuated cowboy, he spoke with a heavy Texan drawl, spacing out his words between long pauses and showers of aws and ahms. He had also cultivated a Southern colonel style of manners, particularly in evidence, I was pleased to note, where Serena was concerned.

During the ten minutes it had taken for the party to assemble I had allowed myself to sail through one of those happy little daydream sequences concerning my first encounter with this J.K. Farrer. It was not that I had any personal designs on him, but the grinding obsession with furthering one's career rarely lets up, even during a holiday weekend, and in my dream he had strode into the room in precisely this way, had taken one look at me, realised that retirement had been premature and that I was the star he had been searching for all his life and had instantly started ringing up millionaires, to get his next great epic on the move.

Admittedly, there was some conflict of interest between this and the other private fantasy, whereby Serena was re-installed as lady of the manor, but as it turned out there was no need to wear myself to a rag deciding between their relative importance, because neither Serena nor I really got a look in when it came to competing for Jake's attention and the instant he discovered that I could not tell a hoof from a fetlock he virtually lost interest in me. Lindy fared slightly better, getting off to a good start by confessing that she was crazy about horseback riding. I suspect that she was equally ignorant on the subject of five-year-olds and equally reluctant to learn more, but she managed to conceal her boredom with a more soulful expression and the suppressed yawns, which occasionally tightened her mouth, as he listed the virtues and defects of his new steeplechaser, were swiftly transformed into little gusts of delighted appreciation.

Primrose, however, was his principal target and they seemed beautifully content to tell each other all over again what they had done together during the previous forty-eight hours, re-stating opinions they had stated at the time and congratulating each other on the acumen each had displayed. This performance aroused a faintly puzzled, but nonetheless respectful attention from Pelham, while Serena, watching it all as the needle dipped in and out, looked as though she were about to burst into song. Any clairvoyants among us would have needed to be on their toes to catch even a whiff of the calamities in store.

That the first thing to go wrong should have been the sirloin was particularly unfortunate, both on account of the prevalence of the American way of life among us, and also because it could so easily have been avoided. Serena had been in such a dither of happiness during the pre-dinner session that she had failed to herd us into the dining room until at least ten minutes after Mrs Thorne had given the signal to go. Moreover, still under the influence of this trance-like mood, she had allowed the schedule to get even further knocked about in the first course, when Jake had gone drooling on about some boring experience he had had in a Moscow hotel, with the rest of us simpering and twitching and casting anxious looks at our empty soup plates. It was a round table, so no one could jump up and start removing them, in pretended ignorance of one being still untouched.

Pelham was invited to carve and he stood at one end of the sideboard, with Primrose at the other piling up a tray for Nannie, and his voice carried less and less conviction as he asked us whether we preferred it well done or rare.

The answers varied a little, but the end product was the same in every case, crumbling chunks of brown boot leather.

The conversation had been general during this operation and so was the silence which followed it. Serena made a few tentative efforts to start the ball rolling again, but no one threw it back, mainly I imagine because we were all equally intent on maintaining the balance between eating enough broad beans and new potatoes to stay alive, and leaving enough to camouflage the uneatable beef.

In desperation, she embarked on a course which presumably she would have seen the folly of, had the situation been a trifle less tense:

'Oh, by the way, Tessa,' she said brightly. 'Weren't you going to tell me what happened upstairs this evening?'

I opened my eyes as wide as they would stretch, registering blankness, shot through, as I hoped, by a subtle gleam of warning, the latter passing unnoticed, however, for as though goaded beyond endurance by this universal lack of support she said impatiently: 'Oh, you know, didn't you say something rather amusing had cropped up while you were dressing for dinner?'

As it happened, I had not said anything of the kind, but considering that I should only worsen matters by arguing about it, I replied:

'Oh, that? Well, it wasn't so desperately funny. Just that the missing spectacles have been found and restored to their owner.'

'Well, that's good news! Where had the poor old silly put them?'

'No one has any wine,' Pelham said, bounding up and crossing to the sideboard to collect a fresh bottle, carefully scrutinising the label before he brought it to the table. 'Where did you get this one?' he asked, refilling Serena's glass. 'Rather going it a bit, aren't you, old lady?'

'What is it? Let me see, Pelham! Oh dear me, no, that never came out of my store cupboard. How could I have drunk a glass of it without realising that? Now, I wonder who we have to thank? Not you, by any chance, playing Santa Claus, was it, Jake?'

'Well now . . . um . . . aw . . . ahm . . . must allow me my ar . . .'

'You're much too generous, my dear, and all your good deeds done by stealth! You don't even give one a chance to say thank you.'

Naturally, I had hoped that this diversion would effectively smother the subject of Nannie and her spectacles, for Primrose had left the dining room door open and I considered that the least said about it the better while Mrs Thorne was in earshot. However, to my intense annoyance, the little murmurs of gratitude and appreciation over the claret petered out into another silence and Serena broke it by saying in a tone of command:

'Well, come along, Tessa, what about the rest of the story? There must be more to it than that?'

This time it was Jake who came to my rescue:

'You know,' he began in his ponderous, gravelly voice, prefacing every second word with a whole spate of ahs and ums, 'the greatest . . . single . . . impact on . . . returning to . . . this country is this fantastic . . . dichotomy . . . of attitudes.'

This led him into a most detailed and tedious exposition of the public concern for pollution, inflation, social unrest and a few dozen other undesirable things, as compared to the private individual's preoccupation with life's trivia, for all of which I felt excessively obliged to him.

'I so agree,' Lindy informed him earnestly, placing her elbows on the table and her palms together in a suitably prayerful attitude.

'What happens,' Jake continued, ignoring her intervention, 'is that the ahm ahm ar entire world is . . . ah . . . in turmoil . . . and we sit here . . . ar um . . . worrying about whether some . . . ah old woman gets ar ar ar spectacles back. I don't know ah whether to call that beautiful or just plumb crazy,' he admitted, finishing with a burst of speed.

No one seemed ready to help him resolve the problem and Serena frowned and said with the utmost seriousness:

'Well, I expect film directors and people like that have a truer sense of proportion, but I don't see how you can be expected to cope with the major problems of life when so much time has to be devoted to the minor ones.'

'Besides, the minor ones are so much more interesting,' Pelham said.

This observation reminded Jake of another utterly pointless anecdote concerning his gamekeeper, in which the latter was quoted verbatim, so that we not only had to suffer all the ahs and urns, but also a very embarrassing imitation of the Herefordshire dialect as well. Fortunately for his captive audience, Primrose returned at around the halfway point and revived the party into a state of startled alertness by digging into her congealed roast beef and polishing off the lot in five minutes flat.

'That's better,' she announced, laying down her knife and fork as Jake paused for breath. 'I was jolly peckish. Anyone want some more?'

'No, thank you, darling, we've all finished now. If you'd just take a few plates out and ask Mrs Thorne for the pudding?'

'Nannie wouldn't touch hers, by the way,' Primrose said, lumbering up again. 'Chucked the whole lot back at me. Got one of her indigestion bouts coming on, by the look of it.'

'Oh dear!' Serena murmured, looking more distressed than the news warranted and so no doubt confirming Jake in his views. 'How very unfortunate! But please keep it dark from Mrs Thorne, will you? We don't want to upset her and I expect Nannie will be able to manage a little caramel custard.'

'Are you joking?' Primrose asked, leaning her weight against the swing door to the kitchen. 'Caramel custard, my foot. She's heard there's gooseberry tart on the menu and she can't wait to get at it.'

'Oh dear!' Serena said again. 'That doesn't sound very sensible. How on earth does she get to hear of these things, I wonder?'

'See what I mean?' Jake asked, looking in triumph from Lindy to me.

'Yes, and I do apologise, Jake,' Serena said. 'I can see that it all sounds very trivial and unimportant, but she does have these awfully bad attacks sometimes and I should have thought gooseberries were the very thing to bring one on. I wish I could spend more time concentrating on pollution and everything, but it's going to be even harder to do, if I have to sit up half the night nursing her through an attack.'

'I guess you've had your share of the big tragedies too?' Lindy remarked rather unexpectedly.

'Well, yes, I suppose so,' Serena replied, flushing slightly and glancing at Pelham. 'No one can expect to get through life without a few knocks; but they don't immunise one against the pinpricks.'

'And Robin is spending the weekend investigating a particularly foul murder which took place only ten miles from here,' I put in, backing her up. 'No one expects us to take a vow of silence while he does it.'

'Besides, it's a ridiculous argument,' Pelham said, joining in the onslaught. 'My dear old boy, you don't seriously imagine we spend all our time frolicking around in Dingley Dell, wearing ourselves to rags over whether to have Sally Lunn or muffins for tea? Even this little backwater has its murky stretches, you know. I can remember some hideous scandals in my youth. Make your hair curl, I shouldn't wonder.'

'Like the baker ar ar aaaarm running away with the candlestick maker's wife?'

'Oh, plenty of that; plus a fair share of the rapes and murders too. Do you remember that awful business of the boy, Serena?'

'Boy?' she repeated vaguely. 'What boy are you speaking of Pelham?'

'Oh, surely you remember? It was the big sensation of the year. I mean the boy who was tortured and left to die, right here in the Park.'

'My dear Pelham,' she asked, staring at him with fearful astonishment, 'how on earth did you come to hear about that?'

'Same way as you, I daresay. Servants' gossip and all the rest of it.'

'No, no, you're quite mistaken, but please let's not speak of it now.'

'Just as you like. Perhaps I've imagined the whole thing.'

'Why no,' Lindy piped up. 'I remember you telling me, Pel. It certainly seemed real enough, the way you described it.'

Serena looked from one to another of them, still shaking her head in a stupefied way, which gradually had a hypnotising effect on the whole table. The spell was broken by the appearance of Primrose in the open doorway, carrying a tray, which she slammed down on the sideboard, saying stonily:

'Every word can be heard in the kitchen, you know. Luckily for you, Mrs Thorne is on the deaf side, but you'd better watch it. I'll be upstairs if anyone wants me.'

She then banged out of the room again, kicking up the door hook with such violence that it went on swinging back and forth for several seconds after she had left.

'I do apologise,' Serena said, almost in tears, 'but we've got on to a painful subject, as you've probably realised. I'll explain why later on, but for various reasons this is not the time for it. Now, who's ready for some gooseberry tart? Not you, Jake, I know, but we've got an alternative. Tessa, darling, I wonder if you'd be kind enough . . . ?'

I jumped up instantly, but Jake was ahead of me, already on his feet.

'Pardon me, Serena, but if I understand you correctly, oughtn't one of us to aw ar go after ah um Primrose?'

'Oh no, my dear, I should leave her alone. I expect she's gone to see Nannie. She'll be back soon.'

'Didn't look quite that way to me. If you'll ah care to excuse me, I'll go and check on it.'

'You must find us somewhat eccentric,' Serena sighed, looking round at her depleted party. 'You, especially, Lindy; but we don't usually behave in this fashion. Bear me out, Tessa!'

'My darling Serena, you make me feel like the utmost heel,' Pelham told her, pushing his plate aside, in order to lean forward and clasp her hand. 'Obviously, I've plunged my tiny foot straight into it. It was quite unintentional, but I should be the one to apologise, for upsetting everyone and spoiling your lovely dinner. Can we please now forget the whole subject and never refer to it again?'

'No,' she replied firmly, 'I think we shall need to refer to it just once more, before it's forgotten. You're entitled to an explanation for our somewhat dramatic reactions, but I'd prefer not to give it to you here, or when Primrose is with us. Not that that need delay us for long. Jake was quite right, of course; she's badly upset and, judging on past form, she won't be coming down again this evening.'

'My God Almighty, I really have set a cat among the pigeons, haven't I?'

'Yes, my dear, I have to agree, and precisely for that reason the matter had better be cleared up once and for all. There's one point I want you to explain for me in return. In the meantime, though, who'd like some more to eat?'

Ironically enough, the pie was delicious, and so was the stiff, yellow home-farm cream which accompanied it, but none of us took up her offer. If my own reactions were anything to go by, we were all too eager to hear Serena's tale to have much appetite left for food.

CHAPTER SEVEN

'YOU may as well hear this too, Jake,' Serena said, when, minus Primrose, he joined us for the after dinner coffee session. 'It does concern you, in so far as it's part of Chargrove history, and one still occasionally hears allusions to it among the people employed here. Besides, it's only fair to Mrs Thorne, now that we hope to be seeing quite a lot of her. One wouldn't want anything said, through ignorance, which might upset her.'

I was privately of the opinion that not upsetting Mrs Thorne was Serena's primary motive in her determination to reveal all, and Jake may have shared it, for he glanced at his wrist watch, which resembled a ship's compass in size and complexity, and said in his harsh growl:

'Well, look . . . ah . . . now, Serena. I have an . . . ahm . . . early start tomorrow . . . If you'll forgive me, I need to get some ar ar ar ahm sleep.'

'This won't take long and we can begin as soon as Pelham comes back. He has gone to say goodnight to Nannie; it was better to get that over first and this may be my only chance. Where is Primrose, by the way? In her room?'

Jake allowed himself about five minutes to answer in the affirmative and at around the halfway mark Pelham returned and poured himself some coffee.

'I must congratulate you, my dear fellow,' he said. 'Not only the best tenant that God ever breathed life into, but you appear to be among the select few in making a deep impression on Nannie. She was positively over-awed by your delivering her dessert in person. The archangel Gabriel couldn't have caused a bigger sensation.'

'I'd say that was . . . ah . . . ah . . . slight exaggeration. Fact is, I . . . um . . . ar . . . often find time to look in for a chat with ah ah . . . ah . . .'

'Just a minute, both of you,' Serena cut in, putting an end to this fruitless exchange. 'Jake's in a hurry and there's something I want to tell you all, before he goes. May I please begin?'

Pelham nodded, without much enthusiasm, and sat down in the armchair opposite hers. Lindy, who was bunched up on the hearthrug, hugging her knees, leant her head against his legs in an attitude of child-like love and trust.

'To understand the background,' Serena began, 'I must explain that Mrs Thorne was in service at the big house when I was a girl, and a very pretty creature she was too, in those days. She married Ted Thorne, one of the under-gardeners and Rupert gave them a cottage on the estate, where they still live. Their boy, Alan, was born about four months after the wedding, which is around average in these parts. It was a long and difficult confinement and she was ill for weeks afterwards with puerperal fever. As you may know, this can temporarily affect the mind and one of the symptoms in this case was to turn her right off the child. Even when she had fully recovered she never had any genuine fondness for him. She brought him up as efficiently as she knew how, but without love or affection.

'You must bear with me if much of this seems irrelevant to you,' she went on, looking down at Lindy, who was picking out pieces of embroidery silk which had become embedded in the carpet and rolling them between her fingers. 'It is important, in view of what people said after the tragedy. And a further point which has to be made is that, maybe as a direct result of his mother's lack of feeling for him, poor little Alan grew up to be a particularly detestable child. Not only physically stunted, but greedy and sly as well and with a kind of cringing manner which made even quite civilised people want to strangle him.'

'Which one of them eventually did?' Pelham asked.

'No, it wasn't as simple as that. The crisis came just after his eighth birthday, which was in late December. It began to snow around midday, I remember. Mrs Thorne was working here in those days and Alan was in and out of the house rather more than she liked, helping himself to mince pies and trinkets off the Christmas tree whenever her back was turned and generally making a nuisance of himself. It wasn't really his fault either. His father was working too and it was the school holidays, so he was thoroughly at a loose end and ready for any mischief. I ought to have stepped in and taken a hand myself, I suppose, but I was younger then and more self-centred, and Mrs Thorne has always been very proud. She would never have stood for anything in the nature of criticism or interference.

'Well, anyway, on that particular morning Alan had been playing her up so badly that she finally lost control and gave him a whacking, whereupon he ran out of the house, howling at the top of his lungs. It was all rather distressing, but unfortunately not specially unusual and I must confess that my chief reaction when he didn't come back was one of profound relief.

'Mrs Thorne left here soon after twelve to go and see to her husband's and Alan's dinner and she was supposed to return at half past two, to wash up and finish off one or two jobs. She didn't turn up, but I hardly registered the fact because by then it had become just another small annoyance in an exceptionally trying day. I was to drive Primrose and Nannie to a children's fancy dress party over near Ledbridge and I was getting worried about the roads because the snow was beginning to come down quite heavily. As though that wasn't enough, there were blood-curdling squalls going on in the nursery, where Nannie was trying to coerce Primrose into dressing up as the fairy queen. As you can imagine, that wasn't a very popular move, and I must say Primrose had my sympathy because no costume could have been more inappropriate. But she had been very naughty and run away and hidden and Nannie had been searching high and low for her, so that the issue had become a sort of challenge to her authority, and I should only have made matters worse by taking the child's side. And so there we were, a most unhappy little trio, including a solid, red faced and tearful fairy queen, setting off at three o'clock for the party.

'It was a ten mile drive and the original plan had been for me to stay and have tea with half a dozen other far flung parents, rather than do the journey four separate times, but the light was already fading when we arrived and our hostess advised me to turn the car round and drive straight home, saying that she would keep Primrose and Nannie for the night. I must admit that I was enormously relieved because I had been dreading the drive home in the dark and also I could now look forward to a quiet evening on my own, which was about the greatest luxury life had to offer in those days.

'Not that I got it, by any means. In the first place, the car went into a skid when I was nearly home, about half-way between the lodge gates and this house and it landed up sideways in a snowdrift.

I had some sacking and a spade in the boot, but the back wheels were wedged right up against the bank and although I struggled for about twenty minutes I simply couldn't manage to free them.'

At this point in the narrative Lindy shifted her position slightly, Pelham noticed that his cigar had gone out and Jake permitted himself another sideways glance at his watch. Watching them, Serena said:

'I apologise for so many details, but they are important because, had it not been for these seemingly trivial accidents the ultimate tragedy might have been avoided. So to resume: I was eventually forced to abandon the car and walk the rest of the way home; and anyone who has had to plod through snow in the pitch dark will understand why it took me all of twenty minutes to get there and what a sorry state I was in when I arrived.

'There were no lights on in the house and Mrs Thorne hadn't been back. The remains of lunch were still on the table and the fire had gone out. I was exhausted and soaked through and I decided that the sensible course was to get out of my wet clothes and into a hot bath, before setting to and clearing up the mess.

'While I was in the bath I heard sounds in the kitchen, so, concluding that Mrs Thorne had come back at last I took my time. However, when I eventually came downstairs I found that it was Ted Thorne who was waiting for me in the kitchen. He told me that Alan was missing. He hadn't come home for his dinner and no one had seen him since his mother sent him packing in the morning. Ted wanted to know if I could throw any light on it.

'Naturally, I was horrified and I immediately asked if he had been in touch with the police, but he said they had thought it best to wait until they had spoken to me. He had tried to ring me up at the house where the party was being held, but they'd told him I was on my way home, so he'd waited until he saw the lights go on here and then he'd come over.

'Incredible as this must sound to the rest of you, and I am sure things have changed a lot now, Pelham will bear me out when I say that, even so recently as that, people like the Thornes who'd been born and brought up on the estate had an almost instinctive habit of shifting their responsibilities on to the people they worked for. Of course there were tenants up at the big house and it was all right to use their telephone, but no one would have dreamt of asking their advice. That could only come from one of the family.

'Anyway, I said that the first thing we had to do was to inform the police and that was where we got caught in yet another maddening delay, because my telephone was out of order. We discovered afterwards that the weight of the snow had brought one of the lines down, but at the time it felt like living through one of those nightmares where you have to struggle to set one foot in front of the other. Luckily, Ted had his car outside and we drove up to the big house to telephone. After that he took me back to his cottage, where we waited until the police arrived.'

'And was there anything they could do when they did come?' I asked.

'Very little. It was mainly a question of trying to reassure the parents. They did get a search party organised and they'd brought tracker dogs, but it was pretty hopeless because, as well as hampering movement, the snow had obliterated scents. Besides, the boy had been missing for nearly eight hours by then and there are fourteen thousand acres on this estate alone; and with no clues to guide them it would have been a miracle if they'd found him. He could have been lying somewhere with a broken ankle, or on a bus to Birmingham, or curled up asleep in a barn not a hundred yards away. I think the police believed that to be the most likely explanation, but they were wrong because the next morning he still hadn't returned and at first light the search began in earnest, with every able bodied person joining in. All the same, it was early afternoon before they found him.'

'Dead?' Jake enquired, having, contrary to all the evidence, mastered the trick of cutting a few chunks out of the script when the need arose.

There was a brief pause while Serena adjusted herself to this jump in the narrative and then she said:

'Yes, and in the most grotesque and horrible way imaginable. He'd been stripped almost down to the skin, leaving him in just his vest and underpants, although they couldn't see that at first because he was completely blanketed in snow. In fact, it was sheer fluke that they found him at all. He was standing upright, you see, lashed to a tree in High Copse, that clump of sycamores above the lake, and to the casual glance it looked as though a pile of snow had drifted there in the wind. It was only because one of the men noticed a finger sticking out that they discovered what was underneath.'

'How horrible!' Lindy murmured. 'How utterly ghastly! Pelham, how come you never told me?'

There was nothing wrong with the words, but something out of place in her manner, for her eyes were shining and she was leaning towards Serena in an attitude of thrilled expectancy. Perhaps Pelham was troubled by it too, for he had been fondling her long hair and now gave it a sharp tug, which jerked her head back and caused her to bite her lip in pain or shock, as he said softly:

'Hush, my darling, don't fret. It's over now and it all happened a long time ago.'

'Yes, it was ghastly,' Serena agreed, 'and I daresay that by some standards it was a long time ago, but although we don't speak of it any more, it's still very much alive in people's minds around here. That's why you must understand that it's not a subject to be treated lightly and why I wanted you to hear the full story.'

'But we haven't heard the full story yet, have we?' I asked. 'There must be more to it than that; like who did it and why. Was he killed first and then tied up?'

'No, and he hadn't been assaulted in any way. He died quite simply from exposure.'

'Why, that's really terrible,' Lindy said, sounding more controlled now, but still over eager. 'When you imagine someone dying slowly like that . . .'

'It's best not to try to imagine it,' Serena said sharply. 'It was not my intention to harrow you and anyway what you say is not necessarily true. It may have been a slow death, but the doctor assured us that he would have lost consciousness quite early on. It would have been more like falling asleep, he said.'

'And did they ever find out who did it?' I persisted.

'Nothing was ever proved, although there were theories galore, as you may imagine. I don't think anyone actually suggested publicly that his mother was responsible, but I know it's what a lot of people secretly believed. All the old history of her mental breakdown was dragged out again and there was a lot of half baked talk about relapses and brainstorms and all the rest of it, not to mention the well known fact that she had never really been fond of the child. As a matter of fact, poor woman, she did go completely out of her mind after the event and had to spend several years in the asylum, but that didn't do her any good with the scandalmongers. On the contrary, they simply said it proved their point.'

'But you don't believe that she had anything to do with it?'

'No, I do not. She may have neglected the boy sometimes and given him a sharp clip when her patience wore out, but there is nothing deliberately cruel in her nature. She could never have done such a thing.'

Having heard some strange and disturbing tales from Robin on the subject of baby battering, I was not entirely convinced. I knew how quickly the impatient slap could develop into far more sinister practice.

'How about Ted?'

'No, not Ted either. He's a most placid man, even less violent than his wife,' Serena answered, showing that, despite her brave assertions, she also held reservations about Alice.

'Who could it have been then?'

'Well, as I told you, there was a lot of talk, but nothing was ever proved. There were some gypsies camping near the village at the time and one of the more charitable theories was that one of them had been helping himself to firewood and, meeting Alan, had perhaps done this to stop him raising the alarm, not realising of course how long it would be before he was found.'

'But why remove his clothes? That doesn't sound very consistent.'

'It might have been to intimidate him, they thought. As he hadn't been assaulted, there was no question of a sex maniac or anything of that sort, and something which lent colour to the gypsy theory was that the whole clan moved on the next morning. They would probably have done so in any case, once the word got around, whether one of their own people was responsible or not. The police caught up with them fairly quickly, but needless to say they didn't find a shred of evidence. So there the story ends and I am sure you can all see what misery could be caused by dragging it out again.'

These concluding remarks, although embracing us all, were aimed chiefly at Pelham, who gave Lindy's hair another tweak before acknowledging them. Then, having taken his time in knocking the ash from his cigar and speaking very soberly for once, he said:

'Curious, isn't it, how distorted memories become with the passing of time? Obviously, I got the outline of the story in a letter from somebody living here at the time; and yet, because everything about this place is so bound up with my own childhood, that particular episode has found its way into the rest of the lore and become as vivid to me as though I had actually been present. Curious, very curious!' he intoned thoughtfully. 'I should make a lousy witness, shouldn't I, Tessa ducks? Hearsay is quite inadmissible in the British courts, I understand.'

Anybody could have seen that Serena was not wholly satisfied with this explanation, but before she had a chance to comment Jake had taken advantage of the slackening of tension to embark on a round of fervent handshakes and farewells. For a man whose chief claim to fame in his declining years was his longwindedness, he could certainly be quick off the mark when it suited him.

While Serena was seeing him off Pelham and Lindy also drifted away and a few minutes later Serena and I bade each other goodnight outside her bedroom door. She was almost collapsing with fatigue.

'Yes, I am,' she confessed, when I accused her of it. 'It has been a specially trying evening, of course, but I do find myself getting so dreadfully tired these days.'

'And that's not all, is it, Serena? You're worried too, I believe. Has it anything to do with Pelham?'

'Oh, Pelham's a funny one, isn't he? A mass of contra-dictions, really.'

'Is that why you told us the story of the Thorne boy? To catch Pelham's reactions?'

'Partly.'

'And was the operation successful?'

'Not altogether.'

'It was all true though?'

'About Alan? Yes, every word of it, though not quite the whole truth.'

'And you'd have expected Pelham to know that?'

'I expect he did, my dear. Anyway, Tessa, there's noth-ing for you to worry about. Everything will sort itself out, I daresay. You run along to bed now, and sleep well!'

'Oh, I will,' I assured her. 'That's the last thing to worry about.'

CHAPTER EIGHT

1

IT WAS to rank among the more spectacular false promises, for scarcely an hour later I woke in terror from the kind of nightmare that makes one frightened of falling asleep again, only to find that the cries and groans which had haunted my dreams had pursued me into the conscious world. It took a minute or two to grasp that they were coming from another room, considerably longer than that to rouse myself to climb out of bed and investigate.

The only reply to my knock was another volley of groans, so I opened the nursery door and went inside. The centre light , was on and Nannie was leaning back in the chair where I had last seen her, wearing a blue dressing gown, with a grey cardigan wrapped round her shoulders like a shawl and a tartan rug covering her legs. Her complexion was livid and she was clutching her stomach and feebly twisting her head from side to side. Aware though I was of her habit of magnifying the slightest symptom of ill health into crisis proportions, I could not believe that this was a fake performance, still less so when I came near enough to see the terrified, imploring expression in her eyes. It was no time for silly questions, so I put my hand against her forehead, in what I hoped would pass for a soothing gesture, at the same time murmuring some vague phrases of reassurance. Her skin was cold and damp, which alarmed me still further, but endeavouring to speak calmly I said: 'Just try and hold on for a minute, Nan, while I get Primrose to ring the doctor. I'll come straight back.'

Instead of bringing comfort, this seemed only to increase her distress and she began trying to gasp out some words, at the same time clutching my free hand in one of hers:

'Mustn't . . . let . . . happen,' she whispered.

'No, don't worry, Nan, nothing's going to happen. The doctor will be here soon and then you'll be all right.'

Her grip on my hand tightened spasmodically and she drew in a shuddering breath:

'No . . . no time . . . help me . . . should have told them . . . tell Mummie not her fault . . . not my baby . . . should have had a boy . . . not that other one . . . mustn't blame . . . sorry Mummie . . .'

The voice died away and her mouth gaped open. A strange, inhuman sound whistled up from her throat, as her head jerked convulsively backwards.

I had seen more than one corpse in my time, but this was the first to have died in my presence and I think the shock of it must account for what I now perceive to have been a slightly odd reaction. Instead of raising the alarm, I gently withdrew my hand, then crept very quietly back to my room and sat down at the desk. There was a pad of airmail paper inside the brocade blotter and some ball-point pens on the flower painted china tray. After a few seconds' steady concentration I was able to recall and write down the fragments of phrases in the order in which she had uttered them; and having done so folded the sheet of paper, put it in my bag and returned to the nursery.

Nothing had changed, but, seeing it now with a more detached eye, I felt saddened by the indignity her death throes had reduced her to, and pulled the rug up over her knees until it completely covered her. As I did so, something slid on to the floor and I bent down to pick it up. It was a pair of gold rimmed spectacles.

2

The mood of calm efficiency started to thaw round the edges when I discovered that Primrose was not in her room. It was in such a fearful state of upheaval that it was impossible to tell whether the bed had been slept in or not, and although her absence adequately accounted for the fact that no one but me had heard Nannie's cries, it also added its mite to the sensation I had felt ever since setting foot in West Lodge of some sinister element hovering just behind my shoulder.

Serena's bedroom was the next objective, but on my way there I met Lindy emerging from the bathroom and providing yet another shock which, although not comparable with what had gone before, was alarming enough, for she looked wretchedly ill. Her hair was hanging loose, but tucked behind her ears and she was mopping her face with a wodge of paper tissues.

'What's the matter?' I asked.

'Just that I'm going to die, that's all. Sick to my stomach. You finally heard me, I guess? Or don't tell me you're feeling bad too?'

'Do you think it was something you ate?'

'Has to be. God, I never felt so awful in my whole life. This is the third time I've had to get up. What are they trying to do? Poison me or something?'

'Who?'

'Oh, Jesus, I don't know. Forget I said it. You couldn't tell me where I would find something I could take to stop it? I don't see any stuff I can recognise in these bathroom cupboards.'

'Sorry, I'm afraid I can't help, but I'd say you were safer without medicine. The doctor will be here soon and if you really think it's food poisoning you ought to wait for him to treat it.'

She leant against the door frame, pushing back a damp coil of hair which had flopped over her fate and saying wearily:

'My mind's gone atrophied, I guess. Why would the doctor be coming? You mean someone else is sick too?'

'Yes, but I can't explain now. It's Nannie and I've got to talk to Serena right away. You might ask Pelham to get up and put some clothes on though.'

'Oh, Pelham! He's asleep. It'd take a bomb to wake him.'

'Then kindly explode one under him. I think he's going to be needed.'

She stared at me, mute and glassy eyed, then with a mighty effort prised herself away from the door jamb and drooped off to her room, a broken reed if ever there was one. I waited until she had gone inside and then knocked on Serena's door.

This should have marked the end of my responsibility and have allowed me to sink into the passive role of tea maker and errand runner, but there was still some way to go before that stage was reached. As so often in great emergencies, it was the trivia surrounding it, rather than the tragedy itself, which dictated the course of events and the trivia in this instance was that Serena had taken a sleeping pill.

She was lying on her side, so still and waxen that my heart turned over at the sight. Then, moving closer, I saw that her lips were parted and she was breathing normally. I began to call her name, softly at first, then louder and more desperately and finally placing a hand on her shoulder, literally to shake her awake, so that she started up with a cry of terror. Recognising me, she became very incoherent, evidently under the impression that she had overslept. I thought it advisable to let her run on, returning to reality by easy stages, but unfortunately I had left the door open and while she was still babbling away Primrose marched in. She was wearing jeans under a dirty old raincoat and looked very repulsive and pleased with herself.

'What's all the commotion?' she asked haughtily.

And where the hell have you been?' I snapped back, not from any deep curiosity, but because her self righteousness provided an excuse to vent some of the nervous irritation which had been building up over the past fifteen minutes.

'Over at the stables. Something I had to see to.'

'At this time of night?'

'One of the mares is in foal and I'm a bit bothered about her, if you must know. Not that I'd expect you to give a damn.'

'Anyway, there are more important things to discuss at the moment. I've got something very serious and urgent to tell you both, so try and get a grip on yourselves.'

Naturally enough, Primrose's arrival, fully clothed, had done nothing to correct Serena's misconceptions and she had been moving about the room in the purposeful manner of one preparing herself to face another day, but one of my remarks did eventually sink in and she turned and asked in a dazed voice: 'What time is it, then?' before picking up her bedside clock and peering at it in disbelief. 'Only half past twelve? I don't understand. Why are you both here?'

'I'm trying to explain,' I told her, 'but it's not a thing to be thrown at you when you're semi-conscious. I've got very bad news and it concerns Nannie.'

'Good God, why didn't you say so before?' Serena demanded, rather unfairly in my opinion. 'Do you mean she's ill? If so, what are we all standing about here for? This is no time to be worrying about my state of mind.'

'Yes, it is, because there is nothing more anyone can do for her.'

'You don't mean . . . ? My God, Tessa, you're not trying to tell me . . . ?'

'Yes, I'm sorry, Serena, she died about twenty minutes ago. I was with her, but there was nothing to be done.'

'How can you possibly know that? Why didn't you call me?'

'Because then she would have died alone and neither of you would have wanted that.'

'But it's unbelievable! She was perfectly all right this evening. At least . . .'

'I honestly don't know, Serena. It looked to me like a particularly violent attack of indigestion, which could presumably have overstrained her heart, but you'll have to wait for the doctor to tell you. Hadn't you better call him, incidentally?'

I had included Primrose in these remarks, but as she was standing behind me they had been addressed directly to Serena, who had not taken her eyes off me since I made my initial announcement. We were both therefore equally unprepared for what occurred next.

Roaring like a wounded bull, Primrose stumbled past me and flung herself on her knees beside her mother:

'Oh no!' she screeched. 'Oh, poor Nan! What have I done? It's all my fault. Oh, Mum, Mum, whatever shall I do?'

'Now, stop being silly!' Serena admonished her, at the same time mechanically stroking her hair. 'And please don't make a fuss, darling. There are things to see to and we must try and keep calm. The most important thing is to get hold of Richard, but I beg you to stop this nonsense about being to blame. That's not going to help anyone.'

'But it's true. Damn you, can't you understand anything? I should never have left her. I thought she was just making it up to stop me going out. And all the time she was literally dying! Oh God, I could kill myself!'

'Stop this at once, Primrose, do you hear me? I don't know what it's all about and I'm sure you don't either, but you must try and pull yourself together.'

Primrose's response to this advice was the rather discouraging one of a long, earsplitting wail and into this tumultuous and affecting scene shuffled Pelham, wearing dressing gown and pyjamas and regarding us with pouting, bleary eyed disgust.

'I should be infinitely obliged if you would make a little less noise,' he informed us, 'or, failing that, keep the door shut. My wife is far from well and this racket is keeping her awake.'

'Oh dear, I'm sorry to hear that,' Serena replied in a distracted way. 'We must get hold of Richard without any more delay. I suppose you couldn't possibly ring him up for me?'

'Who the hell is Richard?'

'Oh, you know, Richard Soames, Father's partner's son, who took over the practice. It's still the same number, four four one.'

'I daresay it is, but I have no intention of ringing him up. There isn't the slightest need for a doctor. A modicum of peace and quiet is all we ask,' Pelham said, padding out of the room again and shutting the door behind him.

Serena stared after him with a blank and hopeless gaze, but Primrose, having dried her eyes, now blew her nose with a ferocious bellow and launched into an entirely new act:

'Leave it to me,' she said in a hoarse, but nonetheless self-important, voice. 'I'll see to it. He'll probably tear a strip off me when he hears how I went out and left her, but that can't be helped. It's no more than I flaming well deserve.'

3

Alone once more, Serena and I drooped into an uncomfortable silence. Personally, I had become uneasily conscious all over again of the old woman lying dead only six feet above our heads and of the necessity to do something about her, although I had no idea what. Nor did I have any clue to Serena's thoughts during this lull, until she enlightened me by saying:

'The thing to remember about Primrose is that she's really very highly strung. People always assume that because she's such a hefty, outdoor type, she must have the temperament of a ploughboy to match, but it's not true. The slightest thing sends her into hysteria.'

'But this is not the slightest thing, is it? One can understand her losing control now. It must have been a fearful shock.'

'Oh yes, but did you notice how quickly she managed to push it away by making herself the centre of attention? All that nonsense about being to blame, it's so immature, isn't it? Just play acting, really, to avoid facing unpleasant realities.'

I did not argue, feeling that her need was to convince herself, rather than me, and after another pause she went on:

'You know, I sometimes feel that's at the back of her obsession about Chargrove. It's not so much that she loves the place for itself, but it's so much more fun to see herself as the dispossessed heroine cheated out of her inheritance by the wicked uncle.'

'Is that really her view of Pelham?'

'It would be, if he gave her half a chance. Unfortunately for her fantasies, he patently doesn't give two hoots for the ancestral home. He'd be delighted to hand it over to Primrose, I daresay, if she could afford to pay him a decent rent.'

'Well, perhaps one of us could drop a hint as to what is required of him, but in the meantime, Serena, do you think perhaps you ought to go up and see Nannie? What I mean is, I'm not, you know . . . very experienced in these matters, and I may have left undone something which ought to have been done.'

'Oh, do you really want me to?' she asked in a frightened voice. 'To be honest with you, I'd much rather not. I have such a horror of death, you see, specially this kind.'

'Which kind?'

'Oh well, you know, very sudden . . . like a heart attack is bound to be. It comes from being brought up in a doctor's house, I think. Casualty patients didn't automatically go to hospital in those days. Quite often they were brought straight to the surgery after an accident, and one used to see the most appalling sights. I remember one child who'd been run over . . . simply ghastly. There was blood all over the hall.'

'Well, there isn't any blood in the nursery, Serena, I can assure you of that,' I said, wondering if the shock had temporarily unhinged her.

'No, of course not, darling, how could there be? I'm being a silly, hysterical coward, aren't I? Nothing much to choose between me and Primrose, when you get right down to it. I'll just run up and take a tiny peep, to say goodbye as it were, and then it will be over and done with, won't it? After all, you've been through a much worse ordeal than that. Well, thank goodness you were here, that's all I can say.'

When she had gone I remained in the doorway, wondering whether to call on Pelham and Lindy and find out how matters were progressing in that camp, or whether to go down to the kitchen and make some coffee to keep myself awake. I could hear Primrose speaking on the telephone in the hall and before I managed to choose between my two boring alternatives she rang off and came upstairs, two steps at a time.

'Where's Mum?' she demanded, having pushed her way past me into Serena's bedroom.

'She'll be back in a minute,' I said, avoiding the direct answer, for fear of setting her off again. 'Is the doctor coming?'

'Yes, leaving right away, he said.'

'In that case, he might be glad of some coffee when he gets here. Shall we go and see to it?'

'You can, if you want to. The mere thought of it would choke me. Can't expect a clot like you to understand how I feel,' she replied ramming the point home by flopping down on the bed and starting to cry.

I raked up one or two conventional phrases of sympathy, but she ignored them and continued to sob into a rather grubby handkerchief, so I left her to it and went out to the landing again.

This time it was a sound from above which dictated the next move. I heard the lavatory flushing in the nursery bathroom and it grew louder as the door was pulled open.

'Are you all right, Serena?' I called, alarmed at the prospect of yet another invalid on our hands. However, when she came forward and lent over the banister she sounded quite steady and composed, although smelling rather strongly of disinfectant.

'Quite all right, thank you, darling; just tidying things up a little. You didn't tell me she'd been . . . you know . . . ill.'

'No, that's right, I didn't.'

'Poor old thing, it seemed heartless to leave her with all that . . . so squalid, somehow.'

'I was on my way to make some coffee. Is that a good idea?'

'Splendid! What a help you are! How's Primrose?'

'In rather a state, actually. I think you should come and deal with her as soon as you can.'

'Yes, I will. Tell her I'll be down in a jiff.'

She had not made any reference to Pelham or Lindy, but as all now seemed quiet on that front I decided to forget about them as well, and, having passed on the message to Primrose and received an angry snort in response, I pattered down to the kitchen.

4

Making the coffee was more of a chore than I had anticipated. Even boiling the kettle presented problems, for I had overlooked the fact that it had its own private switch on the handle. Having rectified this omission and got things humming at last, I next ran into trouble over the sugar. There was a bowl of the coloured crystal variety among the unwashed after dinner coffee cups, but it looked rather too festive for such a grave occasion. None of the kitchen or dining room cupboards yielded up any alternative, so as a last resort I spread the net over the larder as well. The remains of the gooseberry tart and the jug of cream were there on the marble shelf, covered with butter muslin, but I got a nasty shock when I lifted it up because there was a mouse trap, baited with a lump of cheese, standing between them. It was cold and dank in there too, so I abandoned the search and opted for the coloured crystals, after all.

I was carrying the tray through the hall when the doorbell rang, but it would have been superfluous to change course because before the sound had died away the front door opened and a tall, springy man stepped inside. He was in his late forties, at a guess, but going bald, as I discovered when he removed his flat tweed cap, and he had a long, inquisitive nose, lively brown eyes and an agreeably self-confident manner.

I introduced myself and briefly outlined my part in the evening's events and he patted me on the shoulder, saying:

'Splendid! Excellent! Well done!' as though I were a school-girl boasting about her triumph in the hundred yards free stroke. He then asked me to tell Serena that he was on his way up to the nursery and would report to her later.

I followed him as far as the first floor, but Serena's door was now shut and I had to use a corner of the tray to give it a sharp tap. A moment later she joined me on the landing, closing the door behind her again. I passed on the doctor's message and she said:

'I hope he won't be too long because I'm really worried about Primrose. I'm so afraid she'll make herself ill if she goes on like this.'

'You mean the hysterics are back? I thought she'd cooled down?'

'So did I, but it didn't last. I suppose it was having some-thing constructive to do which had the calming effect, but now we're back to tears and remorse. I don't think it's entirely put on either. She wouldn't go to so much trouble just to impress me.'

'How about a stiff brandy?'

Serena shook her head: 'Straight through the roof, if we even suggested it. Alcohol is strictly taboo. Another of Nannie's phobias and I have a nasty feeling that her law is going to be even more closely observed from now on.'

'Why not leave her alone for a bit and let her cry it out, or whatever the expression is? How about some coffee for you? You look as though you could do with a stimulant.'

'I never felt so drained in my life. Who could ever have imagined only a few hours ago that we'd be in this state? I feel guilty about Lindy too. I know the very least I should do is go and ask how she is, but somehow I simply can't face it at the moment.'

'Forget it. She's got Pelham to look after her.'

'I know, and that's strange, isn't it? I realise he's demented about her, which is as it should be, but wouldn't you think he could spare time to come and give me a little support? Specially as he always made out he was so devoted to Nan.'

'He doesn't know yet that she's dead.'

'Doesn't know? What do you mean, Tessa? He must know.'

'If so, he didn't hear it from you or me. When I bumped into Lindy she was far too full of her own miseries to take in anything else, and if you think back you'll recall that Pelham was just as bad. He simply marched in, commanded us to pipe down and then marched out again.'

'But for goodness sake, what did he imagine we were all doing, sobbing and shouting at each other at past midnight?'

'I wondered about that too, but perhaps that kind of thing is normal practice in California. It wasn't all that late by city standards.'

'Then surely he ought to be told at once?'

'There's absolutely nothing he can do at this point. I should think your doctor could take care of everything quite adequately, by the look of him.'

Incapable of remaining perpendicular any longer, we were sitting on the floor by this time, with the tray between us, like two eccentric picnickers and it was thus that Dr Soames found us when he came down from the nursery floor and nodded reassuringly to Serena.

'I've done the necessary,' he told her, 'and I can see to the formalities for you in the morning. She won't have suffered much and a saint couldn't have taken better care of her than you did, so there's no need to upset yourself and don't let's have any foolish remorse.'

'I don't feel even that at the moment,' Serena confessed. 'Only a kind of numbness. It seems utterly incredible to me, after all these years, that we'll never see her again. And there was no warning, you see, nothing at all to show us there was anything wrong.'

'Ah well, that's often the way with coronary cases. She was all set to get another attack eventually. It was mainly her own fault, you know, that it came sooner rather than later.'

'Oh, darling. Richard, how can you talk like that?'

'Common sense. I'd warned her often enough, as you very well know. She was grossly overweight and sitting about on her behind all day, stuffing herself with rich food at your expense brought its own retribution. Still, even if she'd listened to me it would probably only have made a year or two's difference, so there's no point in going over that again. I'll say goodnight and be on my way, if there's nothing more I can do for you.'

'There is just one thing, Richard. I know it's horrid of me to keep you from your bed any longer, but I'd be truly grateful if you'd take a look at Primrose. I'm worried about her.'

'Taking it hard, is she? Doesn't surprise me. Never mind, I'll soon fix her up.'

Serena led him into her bedroom and I stayed outside, drinking a third cup of coffee, which had an even more soporific effect than the first two. I was packing up the tray when Dr Soames came alongside again.

'Can you spare a minute?' he asked.

'Yes, certainly.'

'Come down to the hall, then.'

When we reached it, he opened his brown attaché case, saying: 'I've given Primrose a sedative. It ought to knock her out for a few hours and Serena should stay with her until she drops off. She might be the one to drop first, by the look of her and that wouldn't be bad either. I'll take care of everything and look in and see them tomorrow. Today, rather,' he added, glancing at his watch.

He had taken a white printed card out of his case and was unscrewing his fountain pen while he spoke.

'What's that?' I asked between yawns. 'A prescription?'

'Death certificate. I didn't like to introduce the painful subject in front of Primrose, but they'll need it for the undertakers. Be a good girl and hang on to it until you get a chance to hand it over to Serena, will you?'

He snapped his case shut and put on his cap while I suppressed another gigantic yawn and I asked him:

'Are you going?'

'Yes. Nothing more to be done here tonight and I've got a surgery at nine o'clock.'

'Poor you!'

'If you take my advice, you'll pack it in yourself.'

'I'd like nothing better, but what about the other patient?'

'Which other patient?'

'Oh, didn't anyone tell you? Well, that's probably my fault. Things have got a bit haywire tonight, but it's the other Mrs Hargrave. You know, Pelham's wife.'

'What's the matter with her?'

'Bilious attack or something. She's been sick several times. Pelham seemed to think she was in a bad way, but that was an hour ago and she may have recovered by now. Ought I to go and find out?'

I always expect doctors to be men of steel, receiving the most horrendous revelations with a plastic calm, but this one did not come up to scratch, for my simple remarks had virtually turned him to stone. Only his eyes retained a vestige of life and he used them to fix me with a long and wondering stare. Then, as movement returned, he very deliberately replaced his cap on the table, opened his case and stretched forth a hand for the death certificate, which he placed inside it. After all that he said:

'I think we'll both go. Be good enough to show me their room.'

CHAPTER NINE

'FURTHERMORE, he absolutely insisted on examining her, despite Pelham's opposition,' I told Robin as we strolled in Chargrove Park on Saturday morning.

He had called me from his hotel at eight-thirty, on the point of leaving for London, but on hearing my condensed version of the events at West Lodge, had signified his intention of stopping off there on the way. I had been rather mystified by this, since at the time Dr Soames had still to plant his bombshell under our feet, and also because I had striven to play down my account to Robin, assuming that he had more important things on his mind. This was not so, however, for, as I was shortly to read for myself in the morning paper a man and a woman had spent the night at a police station, helping the police with their enquiries into the death on the M.6 motorway of Mr Cyril Stott. As the female partner of this pair was named as Mrs Marian Stott, it did not take a genius to see that Scotland Yard's role in the affair was now virtually concluded, or that Robin considered he had earned himself a few hours' grace.

'Why did Pelham oppose it?' he asked.

'I'm not sure. The reason he gave was that Lindy had just gone to sleep and he didn't wish her to be woken up.'

'And why shouldn't that have been true?'

'Perhaps it was, but he stuck to it even after Dr Soames had told him about Nannie and that there was a remote chance that her death had been brought on by food poisoning.'

'How did Pelham take the news, by the way? It was the first he'd heard of it, I gather?'

'I'm not sure that he connected at first. For one thing, Dr Soames referred to her throughout as Miss Childers, which I suppose was natural enough, seeing that she was his old patient and not his old nurse, but it seemed such an extraordinarily coincidental name for one of her calling that in thinking about it I quite lost the thread myself, for a while.'

'No reason why it should have affected Pelham in that way. He must have known perfectly well what her name was. Unless of course,' Robin added thoughtfully, 'you take the view that he's an impostor; that the real Pelham died in a saloon brawl in Backache, Montana, and this man stole his papers and is impersonating him, a sort of Chargrove Tichborne. That's rather your scene, isn't it?'

'Oh yes,' I agreed, 'I think we can assume that quite safely; except that he is at least a British impostor, which seems to make it slightly more excusable; and, to be fair, even the real Pelham might have tripped up over Nannie's surname, after all these years.'

'So what happened in the end? Was he finally persuaded to let the doctor see his wife?'

'Yes, when it had been spelt out for him that she might also be suffering from food poisoning and possibly in urgent need of hospital treatment. In other words, that she might not be so much asleep as going into a coma. Pelham could hardly stand out against that.'

'No, and Soames was pitching it pretty strong, wasn't he?'

'Perhaps he thought Pelham was lying. He may have got it into his head that as well as being an impostor he's also an escaped homicidal maniac who goes around sprinkling arsenic in the sugar.'

'Why that particularly? I mean why does your mind leap to arsenic in the sugar?'

'And I'm quite unable to tell you. There must have been a link somewhere, but if so it's gone again. Or perhaps I simply got the idea this morning from Dr Soames. He certainly seems to think there was something fishy about it, although I don't believe he mentioned any specific form of poison. On the other hand, if there has been some funny business, my money would be on Pelham every time.'

'That seems unfair, since I gather it turned out there was nothing sinister about Lindy's condition, after all.'

'No, or at any rate she can only have swallowed a fairly mild dose, for he said her pulse was normal and there was no need to disturb her. Nevertheless, he insisted on ferreting around in their bedroom and in the bathroom and after that he went upstairs and checked through the nursery wing again. He wouldn't tell us what he was looking for.'

'I think I can guess.'

'Me too, in view of what he said this morning, but it was a complete mystery at the time. It was a shame really, because if I had known what he was after I could have warned him he was wasting his time.'

'How come you were in a position to do that?'

'Because if you and I are on the same wavelength, he was looking for what are politely called specimens for analysis, but the fact was that Lindy had discreetly used the lavatory to be ill in and, in Nannie's case, Serena had gone to work before he arrived. She cleared everything up and then threw several quarts of disinfectant around.'

'Odd thing to do, would you say?'

'No, just natural reflex. She'd spent half a lifetime waiting on Nannie and taking care of her and anyway she can't bear any sort of mess and untidiness.'

'With the unfortunate result that Soames now wants a post mortem, before he signs the death certificate.'

'Yes, and isn't that extraordinary of him? Serena nearly fainted dead away when he came to tell her about it this morning. He blathered on about how it was a pure formality and a safeguard against the thousand to one chance that it hadn't been a natural death, but personally I think it's the most officious thing I ever heard of and Serena told me afterwards that she could never have believed he could be such a traitor.'

'It didn't occur to her that his aim might be to protect her, as much as anything else?'

'No, and I must say it wouldn't have occurred to me. I mean, supposing the thousand to one shot comes off? There'll have to be an inquest, in which he'll testify that at the very least her death had been hastened, and that will mean finding out whether this poison was fed to her by accident or with malice aforethought, and if so who by; none of which is going to be very pleasant for Serena.'

'It is never very pleasant when that sort of thing happens, but on the whole most people prefer it to having an unconvicted murderer on the premises.'

'Most people, but not everyone. Not for example the unconvicted murderer.'

'Who you think might be Serena? I got the impression you were backing Pelham?'

'I still am, one hundred per cent, but that's only a personal opinion and, on the face of it all the cards would be stacked against Serena. She had motive, opportunity, everything. It might never be possible to bring a case against her, or to prove it if they did, but most people would believe she was guilty and that's not a very agreeable prospect, you'll agree?'

'Was her motive really so strong? I know the old nurse was a great trial and created merry hell on the domestic front, but I don't see someone like your godmother committing murder on that account.'

'No, I'm not suggesting she did, but unfortunately there's a bit more to it than that. Take Primrose, for a start.'

'Must I? There could hardly be a less promising one.'

'Exactly. We all know what a creep she is, and where do you suppose Serena lays most of the blame for that?'

'On herself, presumably?'

'Well, that too, of course. I know she does blame her own feebleness in having allowed Nannie to exert so much influence, but that's only with hindsight. In the beginning she was so disappointed not to have a son that the maternal instinct lapsed a bit. Primrose turning out to be such an unattractive lump didn't do much to revive it and by the time she'd acquired a sense of responsibility, as a substitute for affection, the damage was done. Primrose had become Nannie's property and far more devoted to her than to her mother and Nannie knew exactly how to exploit that situation. She'd had years of practice with Rupert and Pelham, when she was up against a brigade of strong minded aunts and poor old Serena was a very weak vessel by comparison. Mind you, I'm not the only one who knows this. There are very few people around here who wouldn't privately sympathise if Serena had finally stepped in and put a stop to it.'

'You really play the devil's advocate sometimes, don't you, Tess? You've almost persuaded me that she's guilty and I can give you another nail for the coffin, if you like?'

'No, I hate, but we may as well know the worst.'

'It could be said that she chose this particular evening simply because the house was full of people, two of them virtual strangers, so that, in the event of things going wrong, suspicion would be spread over half a dozen possible culprits. I suppose one can assume that if this had happened on a normal day there wouldn't have been much speculation as to who was responsible?'

'Oh, I agree, but even that's not the worst of it. This particular occasion wasn't only unusual for that reason. There was an added factor which made it positively unique.'

'Jake?'

'No, although she did rather drag him into the party at the last minute, on a pretext which might sound thin to anyone but me. However, the really sensational bit was that Alice, or Mrs Thorne as we are now required to call her, had returned to the fold. Apparently, she'd been helping out in a kind of undercover way for months, doing errands and jobs at home and so on, but Serena was already worn out and a week of Pelham and Lindy had just about finished her. Mrs Thorne was the golden hope. She was loyal to the backbone and she knew the situation at first hand, so it wasn't too much to hope that she would be able to handle Nannie tactfully. Unfortunately, she is also rather stupid and she seized the first opportunity to bounce into the lion's den and give the lion's tail a naughty little tweak. Needless to say, she soon scuttled out again when she got the full force of Nannie's wrath, and personally I have reason to believe that she had learnt her lesson and would be more circumspect in future; but there were witnesses to the fact that Serena had heard about the incident and one could argue that she was under the impression that drastic steps were needed to prevent Mrs Thorne handing in her notice.'

'Well, you've certainly built up one hell of a case against her. I begin to wonder that you have so little faith in it.'

'For the reason you mentioned. It is simply not in Serena's nature to resort to that particular solution, which is why I consider Dr Soames to be so irresponsible in stirring up the mud. He must know what the consequence will be and how ill equipped she is to face it. She's the kind who drifts through life, perpetually hoping that all the nasty things will have gone away in the morning.'

'That type can be the most ruthless of all when they do make up their minds.'

'Yes, that's what people will say. I don't suppose they could bring a case, but the rumours will fly and it's going to be awfully hard for her to live them down. Honestly, I could slay that Richard Soames. Her father's junior partner too! You'd think he'd have more loyalty!'

'Cheer up! There's always the chance that he's on a false trail. It may still turn out that death was due to a surfeit of gooseberries.'

I shook my head: 'No, I don't think so. I have a terrible feeling he's right, and one reason is that my erratic old subconscious has come to life again and reminded me why I spoke of arsenic in the sugar. Last night, when I was making coffee, I couldn't find any, and yet I know it was there at dinner. It was that soft brown kind and it was in a silver bowl. It probably means that after we'd all gone to bed someone came downstairs and removed it, poison and all.'

We walked on in silence, which was broken by Robin saying: 'Then why weren't the rest of you affected?'

'I've been thinking about that,' I admitted, 'and it's not really so puzzling. I have to reconstruct these things in a visual way and here's what I see: at one point the whole party is collected in the dining room, including Primrose who has just returned from the kitchen. She was the first to go out again and she left in her usual boisterous manner, on the pretext of taking Nannie's tray upstairs, having first thrown a pile of sugar all over it. In fact, she never came down again, so that gets her out of the way. Jake was the next to depart, although he doesn't count anyway because he's diabetic and was eating that custard stuff.'

'That still left three of you, apart from Lindy.'

'Yes, but hang on, because the picture's still unfolding. Now I'm looking at Lindy and she's helped herself to sugar, a good whack of it too, as befits the yum yum, little girl image; but gooseberries are evidently a new experience in her life and after one mouthful she screws up her face and makes another dive for the sugar bowl.'

'Interesting! How about Pelham?'

'That's even more so, because, after all the build up, he didn't eat any pie at all; which can't have been because he wasn't hungry, I might add. Serena took a tiny helping, but she was in a very distrait mood and hardly touched it.'

'Which only leaves you. What happened there? Did some sixth sense come to your rescue?'

'I wish I could say so, but I'm afraid I owe my salvation solely to greed. There was a great jug of that lovely thick yellow cream, you see, and I rather let myself go with it. There are limits though and you'd have to be truly disgusting to want sugar as well. In fact it would probably ruin the whole gourmet beauty of the thing.'

'Yes, well I suppose that opens up a narrow field of speculation.'

'Doesn't it, though? Hard to know where to start.'

'Perhaps with the premise that the poison was really intended for Lindy, and Nannie only got hers by accident?'

'Except that it didn't kill Lindy, or even make her seriously ill, so what would have been the point?'

'Oh, it wouldn't be the first time that sort of thing has been bungled, but there remains the question of who would have wanted to harm or kill her. Only Pelham, surely? And he could have found far less clumsy ways of doing it. On the whole, I think we must take it that she was merely part of the cover up, the plan being that at least three people should develop mild symptoms of poisoning, so that Nannie's attack would be seen as part of the pattern, the only difference being that it proved fatal, on account of her age and condition.'

'We progress,' I said. 'We have found out who our intended victim was and that up to a point the plan succeeded. Unfortunately, it doesn't bring us any nearer to naming the culprit, although I suppose we can eliminate Jake, which is rather disappointing in a way.'

'Why is it?'

'Oh, mainly because he's the great outsider and it's always fun when they come romping in ahead of the field. Besides, if the poison was in the sugar he's such a suitable candidate for the job. There was no risk of his being offered any and I should think it might be almost instinctive to choose that particular method, wouldn't you?'

'So why eliminate him?'

'Because he must surely be the one person who had no opportunity to doctor the sugar, or to remove it later on. He went home quite early, probably even before Mrs Thorne.'

'Could he have got back into the house after you were all in bed?'

'Yes, I expect so. Primrose took it into her head to go calling on a pregnant mare and she's more than capable of leaving the front door wide open. In any case, I don't think much locking up goes on in that establishment. There's nothing valuable enough for the professional thieves to bother with and it's too far off the road to attract a casual breaker and enterer. I can't see Jake having any difficulty there, but it still doesn't explain how he could have got at the sugar in the first place.'

'Slipped into the house at some quiet moment during the day, perhaps?'

'No, because he and Primrose didn't get back from Newmarket until tea time, which was after I arrived. The whole party was on the premises then, and Mrs Thorne turned up soon afterwards, so there wasn't a moment when he could have come into the house unobserved. He's about nine feet tall and not easy to miss. Besides, why should he have got his knife into Nannie? Still more to the point, how could he ensure that the sugar would get to her at all? The gooseberries were a very last minute addition to the menu. No, despite my preference for the outsiders, I had to admit that this one is a non-starter.'

'Never mind,' Robin said. 'We've cleared some of the ground. At least you now only have four suspects to choose from.'

'Why four?'

'Well, you can't leave Serena out simply because she came to your christening, still less Lindy, who got a dose of the same medicine. You wouldn't be taken in by an old trick like that?'

'Certainly not, but I wasn't thinking of them. It's more a question of which one you left out. Probably the most important of all.'

'I won't ask who that is,' Robin said, perhaps feeling that he had humoured me enough. 'Then if it does turn out that you have a murderer in your midst, you can have all the fun of pretending you knew who it was from the start.'

Rather put out by this somewhat patronising attitude, I was tempted to lay all my cards on the table there and then, and it would have saved a great deal of trouble for some of us if I had.

CHAPTER TEN

THE result of the autopsy was made known to us on Saturday evening, whereupon Serena, who had spent the day looking as though she were ready to sink into her own grave, perked up in no uncertain manner. While not precisely humming a merry tune, she had the air of one from whom a great burden had been lifted.

There was no obvious reason for this, for Dr Soames's suspicions had been amply justified and there now remained no possibility of Nannie's death having been due to natural causes. However, she explained to us that it was the type of poison involved which made everything all right and proved conclusively that it had been due to a very sad accident.

He had come in person to break the news, in an interview at which Serena, then still in a state of utmost gloom, had begged me to be present.

'I suppose there is no harm in your hearing it too,' he agreed reluctantly. 'It is bound to come out now, but I hope I can count on both of you not to say a word to anyone before the inquest.'

'And what is the word?' Serena asked in a faint voice.

'Death by poisoning, as I had feared all along. Not in a large enough quantity to be fatal in the ordinary way, but quite sufficient in her case.'

'What kind of poison?' I asked, since Serena now seemed incapable of putting the question into words.

'It is called Warfarin. Principally used for the extermination of rats and mice.'

It was this simple statement which brought about the phenomenal change in Serena's mood, causing her to drop back in her chair as tears of relief clouded her eyes.

'Oh, thank God, Richard! Thank God for that!'

'You see it as something to be grateful for?' he asked in understandable surprise.

'Yes, in a dreadful kind of way, I do. Poor old Nan! I can't bear to think of her suffering, but just imagine how much worse it might have been! Oh, you'll never know how worried I was! I was so afraid, well, you know, that someone had made a hideous mistake and we'd never find out how it happened, and then all that terrible business would start up again.'

'What terrible business?' he asked, still more at a loss.

'Oh, you remember all the malicious gossip there was when Alan Thorne died? It went on for months and all it did was to bring misery to innocent people. I felt I couldn't live through an experience like that again.'

'There is no reason why you should have to; there is no similarity whatever between the two events. Unless of course,' Dr Soames went on, now looking almost bug eyed with astonishment, 'you were implying that, having accused Alice Thorne of murdering her own child, people would now say that she had put poison in Nannie's soup?'

'No, nothing quite so blatant as that, but the shadow of such a thing had been looming over me, I do confess it. Poor creature, she's always been so stiff and reserved, more so than ever since her breakdown. People imagine it's either because she's wrong in the head or thinks herself too good for them and everyone knows about the feud between her and Nannie. Unfortunately, poor old Nan was one of the worst offenders in that business with Alan. She said some very unkind things and it wouldn't surprise anyone if Alice had nursed a grudge all these years.'

'Well, I'm with you up to a point, Serena, but being a bit run down as you are, I think you've allowed yourself to make too much of it. What I can't understand though is why you now feel so certain that all the dangers you've been talking about have passed. What on earth difference can it make what sort of poison was used, so long as it was easy to get hold of?'

'Oh, all the difference in the world, my dear. You may not be aware of this, but Nannie had an absolute phobia about mice. It was one of the ways she managed to make life so difficult. She was always nagging me about the house being over-run with them, and it was also her excuse for keeping a private store of food in the nursery, although I've always believed the real reason for that was to give herself all those little between meal snacks.'

'So?'

'Well, don't you see that the one infallible way to attract mice is to keep unwrapped food in a cupboard? Of course they got in all the time and her way of coping with it was to put down masses of this Warfarin stuff you've been talking about. I always thought it was dangerous. She kept a great tin of it on the toy cupboard. You must have seen it there, Tessa, when you were talking to her before dinner yesterday?'

Dr Soames glanced at me enquiringly and I nodded back. I should probably have done so in any case, but it happened that Serena had spoken no more than the truth.

'So you think that through an oversight, some of this stuff got mixed into her dinner? Isn't that rather stretching it?'

'Ah, but you see, Richard, she hardly ever went to bed without eating a last, late night snack. She maintained she couldn't sleep on an empty stomach, if you please, and it usually took the form of a bowl of cereal, with lots of milk and brown sugar all mixed up with some kind of wheat germ which she also kept in a tin on the cupboard.'

'The theory being that she confused one tin with the other?'

'Undoubtedly, that's what happened. They're quite similar, you know, in colour as well as substance.'

'Yes, but even so, my dear, could she really have made such a huge mistake? The poison is very plainly labelled, isn't it? If I remember rightly, there is even a drawing of a vigorous, man-eating rat. She could hardly have missed that.'

'Not in normal circumstances, I agree, Richard, but there's something else I haven't told you yet.'

'Then please do so at once,' he said, leaning forward and looking at her with an earnestness I could not quite account for.

This is not a thing I could swear to in a court of law, but it seemed to me then, as looking back it does to this day, that there was a distinct pause before Serena answered him and that during it she tilted her head very slightly and shot me a warning, or it could have been an entreating look. Then she said:

'She was very independent, you see; hated asking for help, but she was also much more blind than she cared to admit and that night she wasn't wearing her spectacles. She couldn't have been. They were lost several days ago.'

CHAPTER ELEVEN

1

IF DR Soames's disclosure that there was to be an inquest on Edith Mary Childers came as no surprise to any of us, the one which followed it a few hours later amply compensated for that, both in unexpectedness and in its element of grotesquerie. At a small, and up till then subdued gathering at West Lodge after the funeral, Primrose and Jake announced their engagement.

Naturally, given their separate styles of communication, the news was not revealed in one blinding flash. Primrose started the ball rolling in typically inept fashion, having evidently decided to fortify herself for the ordeal by grabbing a sandwich from the tray Mrs Thorne was handing round, with the result that she had her mouth full and those nearest to her were showered with wet crumbs when she bawled out:

'Jake's got something to tell you.'

She then turned scarlet in the face, plumped herself down again and scowled at the lot of us, without any special fear or favour.

There was probably no one in the audience who did not conclude from this introduction that Jake was about to declare his intention of terminating the Chargrove lease and in my own case the impression was actually strengthened when he began to speak. Punctuated by the regulation aw-ing and ahming and laboured sighs, he proceeded to relate in a long drawn out fashion that he had fully intended to end his days in this quiet haven, as a lonely old bachelor, tending his flock and husbanding his green pastures, or words to that effect, but that fate had decreed otherwise and it was now his pleasure to tell us of the great blessing which had been bestowed on him.

Some of the others may have shared my opinion that his timing showed a want of tact, but there was no question that he had gripped our attention. Serena was biting her lip in anguish and even Pelham and Lindy had stopped nuzzling each other. Aware of this, no doubt, Jake manifested a high sense of drama by crossing the room in two manly strides grasping Primrose's hand and announcing through tears of joy that this little girl had done him the honour of becoming the future Mrs Farrer. Whereupon Pelham ruined the scene by bursting into deafening shouts of laughter.

This might not have been so disastrous had not Lindy, ever ready to oblige, echoed him with her own little trills, which so enraged Primrose that she was inspired to make one of the few pertinent remarks of her career:

'Ha ha ha! Very funny!' she said, breathing heavily. 'I bet you find it jolly ridiculous for someone to marry someone twice their age –'

In my opinion, she had scored a point.

'I do beg your pardon, Jake . . . Primrose,' Pelham said, tears of laughter still coursing down his face. 'Of course, there's nothing funny about it. It's the very best thing that could have happened and I hope you'll both be extremely happy.'

'Oh yes, and so do we all,' Serena fluttered unhappily. 'I'm sure we do, but I mean, it's all rather a shock, isn't it? Why did neither of you tell me?'

'We just have told you,' Primrose growled.

'Yes, I know, darling, but you see, you never gave me a hint. I simply don't know what to say.'

'Then simply shut up and say nothing. I don't care.'

'Well, perhaps that would be best. We can talk about it some other time.'

'No, we can't because there's nothing to talk about. We've both made up our minds and you can like it or lump it.'

I doubt whether she would have behaved quite so ungraciously in Jake's presence, but in fact he had already left the room; though not, as it transpired, because he had taken exception to the somewhat tepid reception of his news, but in order to supply the final missing touch in this bizarre situation. When he returned, only two minutes later, he had a bottle of Moët stacked under each arm.

For some reason I could not pin down, this sight evoked a teasing memory, and a sensation of having lived through the scene before which, being so unlikely, made it all the more puzzling. However, there was no time to track it down because fresh diversions were at hand. Admittedly, a funeral party is about the least appropriate occasion yet devised for raising champagne glasses and wishing people long life and happiness, but everything had become so unreal by this time that I daresay we might have taken it in our stride, given a suitable lead from our hostess. Unfortunately, Serena, who normally lived up to her name in the face of fiercest provocation from all sides, let us down with a wallop. Having taken only one sip, her mouth stretched into a grimace, which had no doubt begun life as a smile, and she then quietly dissolved into tears.

At this point, Mrs Thorne, who had been standing by the door, stiff and expressionless as a telegraph pole, darted forward, placed an arm round Serena's shoulder and gently guided her to a chair, while Pelham, Lindy and I hovered uncertainly, looking for something to do with our glasses.

There was a moment of incredulous silence on the part of the happy pair, then Primrose slammed her own glass down, spilling most of the contents on the rosewood sewing table, and barged out of the room. Jake shook his head dumbly, followed up the gesture with a quizzical smile, then realised the act was a waste of time and loped after her, as Serena let out a long, grief stricken wail.

'Oh, my poor child!' she bleated. 'Oh, poor Primrose! What have I done to her now?'

2

'And what had she done to her?' Robin enquired, when I had described this scene to him. 'Did you ever discover?'

'Not exactly. She'd obviously been knocked sideways by the news and was blaming herself for Primrose making such a hash of her life, which is a thing I suppose all mothers are prone to.'

'It sounded more specific than that. As though a fresh element had crept in.'

'And so it has. I suppose the truth is that the poor girl draws some special feeling of security from elderly people and now she's lost her old Nan she wants to be babied by Jake instead.'

'And could Serena be blaming herself for the old Nan's death? Is that what set her off?'

'It wouldn't surprise me, Robin. Serena could find a way to blame herself for practically anything you can name. No doubt, she's now convinced herself that as soon as Nannie lost her spectacles it was her clear duty to lock up every harmful substance in the house. She probably imagines that by neglecting this small precaution she has literally flung Primrose into Jake's arms. Personally, I can't see that it matters if she has. They have loads of interests in common, and when he dies she'll still be reasonably young, as well as rich. There's no reason why she shouldn't live out her dream and spend the rest of her life at Chargrove. Pelham might even be persuaded to get the entail broken and sell it to her. He doesn't want to live there himself and after this weekend I should imagine he'll have even less affection for the place.'

As forecasts went, this was fairly wide of the mark, but in that respect it was modest compared to the one which followed soon afterwards. The conversation was taking place in the parlour and almost as I finished speaking the telephone rang. Through the open doorway I saw Serena coming from the kitchen to answer it and, after the most laconic and unilluminating of exchanges, she replaced the receiver and came to tell us the latest news:

'That was Richard. He says the inquest is to be the day after tomorrow. I wish you could stay for it, Robin. You're such a steady old prop.'

'I know. Isn't it sad? I used to be quite dashing and flighty until Tessa came into my life.'

'Seriously, Robin . . .'

'No, I'm sorry, my dear, but I'm on my way back to London and I have to clock in early tomorrow morning. I couldn't very well ask for compassionate leave on those grounds. The question would inevitably come up as to whether there was no one in your family you could call upon, and I should have to confess that there was not only a grown up daughter on the premises, but a middle-aged brother-in-law as well.'

'And I don't need to tell you what a fat lot of use they'll be. Primrose will probably be carried out in hysterics and it will surprise me if Pelham even bothers to turn up. He can be remarkably elusive when things get rough.'

'Well, at least you'll have Tessa. One could hardly call her steady, but she'll stick around till this is over.'

'You really will, won't you, darling?' Serena asked me.

'You bet! Barring a last minute request to take over the lead at the National, I'm here for the duration.'

'That's a great comfort, and a great weight off my mind.'

This remark would have been even more flattering if she hadn't sounded as though I had still left several tons on it and Robin said in a rather puzzled tone:

'Anyway, it beats me what you're worrying about.'

'As a matter of fact, it was something Richard said on the telephone just now.'

'About the inquest?'

'Yes, and not quite so much what he said as how he sounded. Sort of cross and at the same time embarrassed, the way men do sometimes when they feel guilty. There was something about how I ought to be prepared for a few surprises and he hoped I wouldn't mind too much, but he had to warn me that things might not be quite so straight-forward as we'd hoped.'

'In what way?'

'I simply have no idea. I couldn't make it out at all. Naturally, I was dying to ask him what he meant, but I didn't dare. I had the distinct impression that he had rung me up against his better judgement and that, if I were to press him, he'd get angrier and more embarrassed than ever. I don't think I imagined it.'

'Maybe not, but your mind may well be seizing on details just now and magnifying them out of all propor-tion. You'll probably find that he was in a hurry and had a lot on his mind and I've yet to meet a medical man who hasn't mastered the first requirement of that profession, which is to intimidate the patient who's in the mood to ask a lot of time wasting questions.'

'So you think there's nothing whatever to worry about?'

'Oh, it's possible that some new facts about her case may come to light, but I can't see how they could affect the outcome. After all, you've put forward a very plausible theory as to how she came to swallow the stuff. She was in her eighties and had already had one coronary attack, so Tessa tells me, so I don't see how there could be any argument over the verdict.'

'And you promise me, Robin, that you're not just saying that to cheer me up?'

'No. If he's one of those busybody coroners, he may treat you to a little homily on the carelessness of people who leave dangerous poisons lying around where blind old people can get at them, but I'll practically guarantee that's the worst you can expect,' Robin told her, thereby setting up a new world record for false prophecy.

CHAPTER TWELVE

1

THE verdict, as became inevitable five minutes after the proceedings opened, was Wilful Murder by Person or Persons Unknown, and within forty-eight hours of his leaving the house I was on the telephone to Robin, urging him to return.

'This is a case for compassionate leave, if ever there was one,' I told him. 'The principle object of compassion being myself.'

'Things a bit dicey, are they?'

'Well, naturally, it didn't come as a lovely surprise, or even the sort of nasty little pinprick that Dr Soames hinted at. Serena insists that the whole thing is just a stupid mistake, but the evidence doesn't bear her out and in any case it won't go away just because she refuses to face it. Everyone else seems too shocked or scared even to discuss it. I blame myself too.'

'Whatever for?'

'For not speaking up. I guessed all along there was something fishy about Nannie's death, but you seemed so confident that I thought we were safely out of the wood.'

'What difference would it have made if you hadn't?'

'None to the verdict, of course, but at least Serena would have been prepared. She could have had her solicitor there, for one thing, and between us we might have cooked up a slightly better story than the one she produced.'

'What was wrong with it?'

'Simply that the medical evidence didn't tally in any way with that cosy little theory of her having sprinkled rat poison on her cereal in mistake for wheat germ.'

'Why not?'

'Because, unbeknown to herself or anyone else, except Dr Soames who prescribed it and the chemist who made it up, she'd been taking regular doses of this Warfarin stuff for the past two months.'

'You're joking?'

'Not for one moment. This may come as news to you, Robin, it certainly did to me, but it appears it's quite commonly used in some cardiac conditions. It thins down the blood and reduces the risk of a clot. They don't often give it to old people, but Dr Soames tried it on Nannie as a last resort, because he'd entirely failed to get her to stick to a diet or lead a sensible kind of life. She'd been on it for weeks and there hadn't been any ill effects whatever, so you can see what that means?'

'That she'd acquired a degree of tolerance?'

'Right. In other words, a small amount such as she might have swallowed by mistake probably wouldn't have done her any harm at all.'

'Hang on a minute though, Tessa. You said just now that this drug, or whatever it is, isn't normally prescribed for elderly people, right?'

'Right.'

'So doesn't that mean it can be risky, even in quite small doses?'

'Exactly the point which the Coroner raised and Dr Soames got very peeved about it. Of course his professional reputation was at stake, so he was extra touchy, but he was absolutely positive this didn't apply in Nannie's case. He'd been meticulous about taking blood counts and so on, from the moment he put her on the stuff and he swears that he'd have noticed at the first sign of anything going wrong. In any case, the autopsy showed up a far greater quantity than should have been present in the circumstances.'

'When did he last visit the patient?'

'About ten days before she died. The theory being that during the week before death the intake had been stepped up to about four times the regular dose. We were given a small straw to clutch at when it was put to him that she might have increased it herself, on the principle that the more of this preventive medicine she took the more she could lash into the rich food. That would have been quite in character, but unfortunately it wouldn't stand up. She was on the National Health, so could only get the stuff on prescription and she had to produce a new one each time she wanted a fresh supply from the chemist.'

'In other words . . .'

'Someone else has been systematically increasing the dose.'

'Who collected the medicine from the chemist?'

'Sometimes the doctor brought it up himself. Otherwise, practically anyone who happened to be going down to the village, and in fact I'm sure she won't mind a bit,' I continued, without a break but with an abrupt switch of tone, 'she's always saying how much she wishes you were here.'

There had been a sound on the landing above, followed by Serena's descent to the hall, and I had implicit trust in his ability to catch on. This was not misplaced.

'Have you gone mad or can you be overheard?' he asked.

'Yes, marvellous!'

'Well, I'll do my best for you. It may take a bit of re-arranging, but there's a weekend coming up and I might conceivably wangle an extra day and join you on Friday.'

'Oh, good! We'll expect you about tea time.'

'Don't count on it.'

'Yes, I will. Goodbye, darling.'

2

'The only trouble is,' Serena said, swiftly filling the vacuum left by the removal of one worry, 'I don't know where we'll put him. You can't both squeeze into the boxroom. There's the nursery, of course, but one could hardly suggest his sleeping in there.'

'I don't suppose it would bother him in the least, he's not nearly so squeamish as you or I would be, but I shouldn't dream of letting you put him up. You've got more than enough to do already, without saddling yourself with an extra guest and Robin is expert at finding his way around.

He's bound to get fixed up with somewhere to stay before he leaves London.'

'I suppose we could give him Primrose's room and ask her to move over to the big house for a couple of nights,' she went on, unaccustomed to having problems swept from her path so expeditiously. 'There's really no reason, when they're so soon to be married, why he should be rattling around there on his own, with at least fifteen empty bedrooms, but I'm afraid his old world scruples would prevent his sharing the same roof with the bride until after the ceremony.'

In view of Primrose's moonlight caperings on the night of Nannie's death, I doubted if Serena had gauged that situation accurately, but since it was a question liable to unlock further floodgates of self-recrimination, I chose another one:

'Have they settled the date yet?'

'If so, they haven't told me, but I daresay I shall be the last to hear, since she flatly refuses to discuss it with me. Personally, I should think the sooner the better.'

'Is that so? I had the impression you weren't wholly in favour of the match?'

'I'm not; quite the contrary, but since they are determined to go ahead, irrespective of my wishes, I consider it would be a pity to waste any more time than they need to. How old would you say he is?'

'Sixty-four, according to *Who's Who in the Theatre*.'

'There you are! Not only old enough to be her father; old enough to be her grandfather!'

'Nevertheless, he probably has what one might call a few active years ahead of him.'

'Which was more than Rupert had when we were married,' she admitted wistfully.

'Which just goes to show that picking on someone of your own age is no guarantee of a long and happy marriage.'

'That's not the point,' she snapped. 'Rupert and I were madly in love. If I had to choose again, I'd far, far rather spend one year with him than a lifetime with anyone else. Primrose is quite different. I know exactly what she's after and love doesn't come into it. It's Chargrove she's marrying, not Jake.'

'Whatever her motives, you shouldn't be too discouraged. If she does find the price too high, she can always join the ranks of the divorced wives and live at Chargrove on his alimony.'

'Really, darling, you can be very cynical sometimes.'

'I know, but I always recommend people to settle for half a loaf if it's all they can get, and only the other day you were complaining because there was no husband at all in the offing. At least you've progressed a step or two from there.'

'I'm afraid I can't agree. As you know, I always blamed Nannie for that, and I did believe . . . well, I know it's wicked to wish for anyone's death, however old and useless they may be, or to be thankful when it comes, but I confess that I had allowed myself to hope that it wouldn't come too late for Primrose to break out of her shell and grow up. And so I believe she would have, given time, but now Jake has snapped her up even before she's been able to draw breath and look around. It's too sickening for anything.'

It was also beginning to sound very much as though, in Serena's view, Nannie had died in vain and I was tempted to warn her not to express it too publicly. However, the opportunities for a private talk, such as we were then having, were becoming increasingly rare and there was one much more urgent matter which I needed to clear up.

I was searching for a tactful way of broaching it when, to my disgust, we were interrupted by Pelham. He stuck his head round the door and asked:

'Serena love, what's Richard's number?'

'Four four one. Why? What do you want him for?' she answered in a flutter of apprehension.

'Lindy's being sick again.'

'Oh no!'

'Oh yes! As a dog. Personally, I think we should remove ourselves to London at the earliest possible moment and see a specialist, but she has formed the opinion that the journey would kill her in her present state, so we shall have to make do with the local talent for the time being.'

'What do you suppose it is? Nerves or something?'

'Now whatever makes you say that?' Pelham asked, coming right into the room and closing the door behind him in a faintly sinister fashion. 'What has Lindy got to feel nervous about?'

'I didn't mean it in that sense. More sort of upset was what I meant. After all, it can't be very pleasant for her being thrust into a houseful of strangers and then all these horrid things to happen. Enough to upset anyone.'

'Oh, bosh, my darling! Lindy's totally indifferent to anything which doesn't touch her personally. It's one of her charms. She'd have far more cause to be upset if you were not all strangers.'

'Well, I'm relieved to hear that, but it doesn't alter the fact that she's not well. Do you suppose she could be sickening for something?'

'Now you mention it, I should say that's far more likely. Mumps or measles, I shouldn't wonder. I do hope Primrose has had them all. It would be rather maddening if she were to succumb on her wedding day.'

Evidently displeased by this flippancy, Serena glanced at her watch and said primly:

'In any case, you must try and get hold of Richard right away. He starts on his afternoon rounds about now, but you might just catch him. Or would you rather I saw to it?'

'If you would be such a blessed angel. You know him so much better than I do and one can't deny there was a little coolness last time we met. I was never much good at climbing down and admitting my mistakes, as you probably remember.'

I had moved over to the window while they were hammering this out between them, seeing it as no concern of mine, but now turned round again to deliver a timely warning:

'You'd better look sharp. A car has just driven up and two men are getting out. They look to me strangely like policemen.'

CHAPTER THIRTEEN

1

DETECTIVE Superintendent Hobley-Johnson, supported by Sergeant Kyles, interviewed Serena in the parlour, whence Pelham and I were firmly and politely dismissed. He was a pallid, freckly man, with white eyelashes and rather vacant looking blue eyes, and it must have been the more conventionally attired sergeant who had so clearly proclaimed their profession. The Superintendent wore a check suit and pale suède boots and looked more like a motor salesman trying to look like a Guards Officer. He had manners to fit this dual personality too, for they varied between a somewhat forced geniality and the cool, quiet authority of the born leader of men.

I did not expect either approach to do much to reassure Serena, whose expression, when asked if he might have a few words with her in private, would have been more fitting on the prisoner in the dock waiting for the judge to pass sentence.

Pelham also seemed strangely ruffled and I was amazed to see how little either of them had apparently been prepared for this visit. I should certainly have taken care to announce it less abruptly if it had occurred to me that anyone could doubt, since a murder was presumed to have taken place on the premises, that sooner or later the police would evince some curiosity about it.

'Be a love and ring up the doctor for me, will you?' Pelham called out, galloping up the stairs as he spoke. 'Must go and see how the poor pet's coming along. Shan't be long.'

He was as good as his word and in less than ten minutes was back again, moving at a soberer pace and having combed his hair and put on a tie, as well as attending to the poor pet in the interval.

'All's well,' he said airily. 'She's feeling much better now. A little tendency to hypochondria there, between you and me. She could manage a cup of tea, so cancel the call and put the kettle on, will you, Polly darling?'

'Too late,' I replied, all the more smugly for resenting his assumption that I had nothing more pressing to concern me than his wife's imaginary illnesses. 'He was just going out and he won't be back until evening surgery. He'll try and get here around five o'clock.'

'Oh, will he? How very boring of him! However, I daresay he leaves a record of where he's going. See if you can get his secretary or whatever. She may be able to catch him at some point along the route.'

The odd thing about Pelham was that although on the surface not a highly perceptive man, if he were a fake the impersonation was truly inspired. It was hard to believe that anyone apart from a born and bred Hargrave sibling could display such sublime confidence in my desire to implement his slightest wish. I was debating whether to hand him some story about the doctor's receptionist having gone to the hairdresser, or simply to point to the telephone in a marked manner when the conflict was brought to an end by the parlour door opening and Serena joining us in the hall.

'Ah, there you both are, that's lucky! The Superintendent would like to talk to you, Tessa. You too, Pelham, if you wouldn't mind, but he'd like Tessa to go first.'

'How was it?' I muttered, using the ventriloquist technique, for she had left the door open, but she merely frowned and shook her head, then turned to Pelham to enquire after Lindy.

Ignoring this, he said: 'As it happens, I do mind. There is nothing whatever I can tell him and, so far as he is concerned, I am virtually a stranger in these parts.'

'I can see you first, Mr Hargrave, if that would be more convenient,' the Superintendent said, materialising in the doorway.

'No, it wouldn't, not at all. As I was pointing out to my sister-in-law, I am only a visitor here and I know nothing at all about what happened.'

'Nevertheless, I take it you would not wish to obstruct us in our duty, sir? On the other hand, if you would prefer to call in at the station, when you can spare the time?' the

Superintendent enquired, with an odd mixture of menace and amusement in his voice.

It must have been the menacing ingredient which got through to Pelham, for he dropped his bullying manner and said with a touch of bravado:

'Oh, very well, if it means getting you into trouble with your superiors, far be it from me . . . I'll let you have Mrs Price first, however. My wife is far from well and I must find out if there is anything she needs before you slip the handcuffs on.'

'I shall want to see her as well, as soon as she feels up to it,' the Superintendent called after him, still sounding amused, although, since he was now playing it so cool and canny, softly enough for Pelham to pretend not to have heard him. 'And now, if you'll be good enough to step this way, Mrs Price? I shan't keep you a moment.'

2

It is always hard to assess what people mean to convey by that remark, for experience has shown it to be largely meaningless. It comes into the same category as interrupting someone by telling them that you haven't come to interrupt them.

In this case the moment stretched to approximately a quarter of an hour, with me perched on the green brocade sofa, the Sergeant crouched over Serena's kneehole writing desk, giving the impression that he might shatter it to pieces with one careless stroke of the ball-point pen, and the Superintendent taking no chances and standing with legs apart in front of the fireplace, reminiscent of one just returned from a day out with the Heythrop.

He began with the routine questions, from which it emerged that I was Mrs Theresa Price of Beacon Square,

S.W.1., also professionally known on stage and screen as Theresa Crichton. Evidently, this was not a name he had ever heard of and furthermore there was no sign of his feeling that he ought to have heard of it, so I awarded him nought for diplomacy and we passed on to the next round of questions.

These concerned the duration of my stay at West Lodge and in the process of answering them I contrived to let it be known who had dropped me off there on the previous Friday, and in what circumstances. This brought mention of a name he most decidedly had heard of and I noticed that his shifting of weight from one foot to the other coincided precisely with the moment when our little talk moved on to a new level of mutual understanding.

From this point everything flowed along smoothly, with none of that uncomfortable probing for details which I had secretly feared, and when it came to my account of finding Nannie and of describing her last conscious moments, which was naturally the crux of the interview, I was able to steer a straight and narrow course between two precipices. One of these had been created by his asking whether she had said anything which might have some bearing on the manner of her death and although he put this question in various forms he did not appear to doubt me when I maintained that she had mentioned no names and had said nothing which was really intelligible. There was no reason why he should have, since it was perfectly true, but I hardly felt compelled to add that, having committed them to paper, I could, if he had requested it, have repeated every word she uttered. Goodness knows what he might have made of them, but I was not prepared to risk finding out at least until I had consulted Robin.

The second point of reticence was connected with Serena's evidence and here the form of the questions made it even simpler to draw a few veils. It came right at the end of the interview when, having thanked me for my co-operation and mentioned that I should be asked to sign a statement in due course, he added:

'By the way, Mrs Price, just one other small matter. It has to do with those missing spectacles. I don't suppose you can throw any light on it, for I understand they were lost before your arrival, but you wouldn't have any knowledge of their present whereabouts?'

What I had instead was a direct clue to this part of Serena's statement, enabling me to answer firmly:

'Sorry, no. She did mention to me that she'd lost them, when I was talking to her earlier in the day, and as far as I know they're still missing, but that's all I can tell you.'

This was also true, as far as it went, but he accepted it in such good faith, merely flapping his white lashes at me and saying, 'Jolly good!' in such a very sad voice that it was some minutes before I stopped feeling like a mean, rotten skunk.

3

'So you came, after all?' Pelham said, emerging from the parlour himself about half an hour later and casting one of his haughty and insolent looks at Dr Soames who had just arrived. 'Didn't you get my message? Your receptionist promised to pass it on to you at the hospital.'

'And so she did. In the circumstances, I chose to ignore it.'

'Then I'm afraid you've had a wasted journey. My wife is recovering.'

'I think that is for me to decide.'

'My dear fellow, you can't force yourself on her, if she doesn't wish to see you.'

'Yes, I can,' Dr Soames replied most equably, 'in the circumstances.'

As before, Pelham capitulated in the face of implacable opposition and, putting on a feeble show of being in control of the situation, said carelessly:

'Oh well, on second thoughts, perhaps it's just as well you are here. That bobby in there has had the impudence to say that he wants to interview Lindy. You can tell him that she's in no condition for anything of the kind.'

'I think that will also be for me to decide. Shall we go up now?'

'You know the way,' Pelham said and then turned to vent some of his frustration on me, demanding to know where Serena was.

'In her room, I believe. And, by the way, people don't call them bobbies any more. I doubt if they did, even when you were a boy.'

This, however, was not the kind of thrust to get through his defences.

'We were brought up by a very old-fashioned lady, don't forget,' he said, lifting me into the air, so that my face was on a level with his when he kissed me. 'Come along, let's both go and find her. I have news to impart and little Miss Big Ears may as well hear it at first hand. Or does that expression date me too?'

'Not particularly, although I don't see why you should apply it to me.'

'Oh, I've seen you watching us all, don't think I haven't. Quite unnerving sometimes.'

'Why? Have you got a guilty conscience?'

'What a stupid question for such a bright girl! Do you know anyone who hasn't? I would have expected you to do better than that.'

'All right, try this: tell me in two sentences what you want to say to Serena. In that way I shan't have to listen to the padded out version you'll give her and can transfer my snooping to more rewarding areas.'

'Oh, there won't be any padding out of this one, let me assure you. I simply wish to tell her that as soon as Lindy feels well enough to travel we intend to remove ourselves to London. As my hostess, I consider that Serena has every right to know.'

'Won't you need permission from your bobby before you do that? There's a murder investigation on foot, in case you didn't know.'

'Ah, now you're being stupid again. You really should credit me with a little more sense that to walk out without clearing it with the rozzers. It would be tantamount to an admission of guilt, I daresay. In fact, the jolly old bobby assures me that he hasn't the least objection, so long as I leave my address. Not even required to surrender my passport, you notice? I don't think he can quite be putting his heart and soul into this business, do you?'

'What kind of passport do you hold, Pelham?'

'Now there's a funny question! I wonder what you're up to this time?'

'I simply wondered if it was dark green or dark blue.'

'Ah yes, I follow you.'

'Since you've been pursuing your career in the States for the past quarter of a century, I thought you might have found it necessary to become an American citizen by this time?'

'No, that only happens to people who don't completely know their way around. You still have a lot to learn. And now, if you'll excuse me and have found out enough to keep you happy for a bit, I shall find Serena and break the news. I expect her, and my niece too, to be quite overjoyed, so it seems a shame to leave them in the dark longer than we can help.'

Nevertheless, some further delay proved inescapable because he was only halfway to Serena's room when Dr Soames appeared on the landing and said something which, to my regret I could not catch. Pelham continued on past his original destination, then I heard another door shut and after that silence.

As though he had been waiting in the wings, the jolly old sergeant bobby came out of the parlour and informed me that the statement was now typed out and awaited my perusal and signature.

CHAPTER FOURTEEN

1

PASSING the open nursery door, *en route* for the apricot box, I spied Serena sitting on the floor beside the white cupboard, surrounded by broken, shabby toys and a pile of dusty old 78 records.

'Trying to clear out some of the junk,' she explained. 'Poor old Nan was such a hoarder and anything that one of the children had been fond of was practically sacred. Some of this stuff must date back to Rupert's infancy, by the look of it.'

'Is this really the moment?'

'No, I suppose not, but it more or less crept up on me. I started to clear out a few things and this is how it ends.'

'You weren't looking for her spectacles, by any chance?'

'Not specially. That's a mystery, isn't it?'

'I hope you won't mind my making it still more mysterious. I ought to have told you this before, but there hasn't been much chance and I didn't want to refer to it in front of Dr Soames, or anyone else for that matter.'

'Refer to what?'

'The spectacles. The point is, they were here, in this room, when she died.'

'Oh, my dearest girl, whatever makes you think so?'

'I saw them. They were hidden in a fold of the rug which she'd spread round her legs. When I pulled it up the glasses fell on the floor.'

'But that's incredible! Are you quite sure you're not mistaken? Don't forget that you were terribly confused and distressed at the time.'

'Was I?'

'You certainly appeared so, though I don't suppose you remember much about it now. Merciful, isn't it, how the memory obliterates these unpleasant experiences?'

'Yes, isn't it? Nevertheless, I did see the glasses. I remember bending down to pick them up. They were in my hand.'

'Where did you put them?'

'On the table there . . . I think.'

'There you are, you see!' she announced triumphantly. 'You're not sure, are you?'

'Not about that bit. At least, I couldn't swear to it on oath, but I am positive about the rest of it. If you don't believe me, there's a very simple solution. Why not ask Mrs Thorne?'

'I have. That was the first thing I did, naturally.'

'What did she say?'

'Exactly what you told us at dinner. That she'd found a pair of spectacles, believed them to be Nannie's and had taken them up to her; but you hadn't heard the end of the story.'

'No? How did it end?'

'Apparently, they weren't hers at all, hence all the fuss. Nannie probably saw it as some kind of trick, to tease her, which was why she lost her temper and said such rude things.'

'Oh yes? And then what?'

'That was all. Alice was very upset and she ran out of the room.'

'I mean, what did she do with the spectacles?'

'Oh yes, well, you see, she realised she'd made a mistake and that they must belong to Pelham or Lindy, so she put them back in the spare room.'

'She wasn't carrying them when she came out of the nursery.'

'I expect they were in her apron pocket. What is this, darling? Some kind of inquisition?'

'No, it's just that I'm still a bit puzzled. All these loose ends bother my tidy mind. One pair of spectacles lost, one pair found, but it turns out that they're not the same pair. Now it seems that the first pair is still lost and so is the second pair.'

'No, no, dearest, you must try not to make everything so complicated. That's not the way of it at all. The original pair, as you say, is still lost; those which Alice found must have been left behind by Aunt Louise last time she stayed here. She's another dotty old lady who's forever putting things in a safe place and forgetting where she hid them. That brings us back to where we started and there was nothing odd or sinister about Nannie having mislaid her glasses, I can assure you. She was always doing it and, naturally, without them she couldn't find them. It's perfectly simple, you see; no problem at all.'

'Except, at the risk of being a bore, I must repeat that this time she did find them; or someone else found them and returned them to her, and subsequently that person or someone else saw fit to remove them again after she was dead. One either has to accept that, or else that a third pair has entered the script because, whatever you may say, I did see them, right here in this room.'

'Yes, I expect you did, Tessa, but please don't worry so much about it. I think you've overlooked the most obvious explanation of all and it was silly of me not to think of it before.'

'Well, now that you have, do put me out of suspense.'

'The fact is that we've both been so upset by the inquest that neither of us is thinking straight. You'll kick yourself for not seeing this before, but what must have happened is that the lost pair had been tucked away in the rug all the time. It was the last place that anyone would have thought of looking in and at this time of year she wouldn't have needed to use it very often, so there they stayed until the night she died. Doesn't that solve the mystery?'

'Up to a point. I'm not kicking myself so it hurts.'

'Now, why's that?'

'Well, where are they now?'

'Yes, I know, that is rather peculiar, isn't it?' Serena answered smoothly. 'But I daresay we shouldn't have given it a moment's thought in normal circumstances. Perhaps the undertakers put them inside the coffin. If not, I'm sure I'll find them sooner or later, among all this rubbish.'

It was like trying to lift up a marble with a pair of chopsticks. Each time I raised it up it slid out again, and the longer it stayed aloft the louder the crash as it fell back on the plate.

'Yes,' I sighed, 'if you try hard enough, I feel sure you will. To change to a more fruitful subject, has Pelham spoken to you yet?'

'Not since I last saw you. Why?'

'In that case, he must still be with Lindy and the doctor.'

'No, he's not. Richard left a few minutes before you came upstairs. I saw him from the window. Pelham was out there too, seeing him off. Very civil he was being. The police have gone too.'

'Ah! Well, that probably accounts for Pelham's good humour. He's chivvied the doctor into certifying that Lindy is too ill to be interviewed, no doubt. I'm afraid we haven't seen the last of them, though.'

Serena sighed: 'How tiresome and ridiculous it all is; but I suppose I could have foreseen that Nannie would go on making a nuisance of herself long after she was dead.'

'Well, cheer up, because good news is on the way.'

'I could certainly do with some. What is it?'

'I'd better leave that pleasure to Pelham, but I think you'll be pleased and I'm sure Primrose will.'

'That's the best news of all,' Serena said, her expression lightening for the first time for days. It was a sight I was later to recall with some remorse.

2

Retreating from the nursery, I saw Lindy on the staircase. I think she had been on her way down, but she swivelled round to make it look as though she were coming up.

'Hi, Tessa!'

'Hi, Lindy! Feeling better?'

'Oh, loads. I'm fine now, thank you.'

'That's good. You gave us all a nasty scare.'

'I did? Why? I just felt a little off colour, that was all. Everything's okay now.'

'The trouble is that the current circumstances are not propitious for being off colour in.'

'Oh, I see what you mean. But it wasn't at all that kind of thing. It was just . . . well, it was just nothing, really.'

'Glad to hear it. Were you looking for Serena? She's in there.'

'No. Tell you the truth, I was on my way up to ask if you felt like a walk this fine afternoon? I'm feeling kind of cooped up, being in my room all day.'

It was a reasonable claim and yet, in some indefinable way, her manner did not quite bear it out. Her face, it is true, was rather drawn, making her eyes appear larger than ever, but there was a flush in her cheeks and a hint of bottled up excitement in her voice. Exhilarated, rather than cooped up was how I would have described her.

'Anywhere in particular?' I asked, suspecting that the walk might be the excuse for a private discussion, rather than an end in itself.

It was not so, however, for she climbed a few more stairs, clasped the newel post with her tiny, chicken bone fingers and said in her most babyfied voice:

'You won't laugh at me?'

'I shouldn't think so.'

'Or tell on me?'

'Not if you say so,' I replied, fighting a losing battle with boredom and impatience.

'I wanted to see if we could find where that boy was tied up. You know, the one Serena was telling us about.

She said it wasn't too far from the lake and I thought, if we were together, you knowing the place so well, we might have a chance of locating it.'

'That sounds rather a morbid objective for an afternoon stroll.'

'Oh, sure, but then I am morbid,' she answered cheerfully. 'I have this very, very morbid streak in me.'

'You wouldn't prefer me to try and talk you out of it?'

'Why no, Tessa, that's good of you, but it wouldn't be any use. Lots of people have tried. I even tried it on myself, but it hasn't got me anywhere. I keep thinking about that poor kid all alone out there and what really scares me is that it could get all twisted up inside me, so it would come out some day in a different form and I'd do something awful that I didn't even know I had it in me to do.'

'And we don't want that,' I said. 'We have enough trouble with the people who do know what it's in them to do.'

'So you will come with me?' she begged. 'I have this crazy, neurotic urge to find the place and see it with my own eyes and Dr Soames says I have to face up to my problems, instead of trying to pretend they aren't there. So I want to try and get it out of my system, but all the same I'd be scared to go on my own.'

All this claptrap was thrown out quite matter-of-factly, but with a deadly seriousness that more than half convinced me that she was in earnest. At the same time, there was also the slender chance that, either on her own initiative, or acting on Pelham's instructions, she had some quite different motive for wishing to inspect the scene of this ancient crime. If so, it could only be to my advantage to find out what it was and I said:

'Okay, I'll just get a jacket from my room and I'll be with you.'

'Thanks, Tessa, you're a real sport! See you downstairs.'

'In two minutes,' I agreed.

It was to be hoped that she wasn't counting them because the two minutes stretched to seven or eight before I rejoined her. The reason for this was the rather odd one that as soon as I walked into my bedroom I saw that the centre drawer of the apricot flounced dressing table was tightly closed. Some people of my acquaintance would have been more disturbed by finding it in some other position, so I must now confess to an idiotic but deep rooted superstition.

At the age of about eighteen I happened to be doing some practice make-up one afternoon when the telephone rang, and the ensuing conversation had led to my very first engagement in the theatre, which happened to be A.S.M. and understudy in a pre-London try-out which never got further south than Macclesfield. Some minutes after replacing the receiver I had drifted gracefully down from the clouds and had noticed that my dressing table drawer, for reasons now forgotten, was wide open. I was about to close it with a joyous slam when it flashed into my mind that this was the good luck position for it to be in and, so far as humanly possible, I have never completely shut one from that day to this.

Naturally, I soon discovered the impracticability of going through life leaving a trail of wide open drawers in my wake, so over the years I have developed a technique whereby the principle is upheld, without incurring the slur of eccentricity, and nowadays the drawer is always left open a token two inches.

Normally, this is scarcely noticeable by me or anyone else, but in Serena's apricot box it had been sufficient to cause a distinct bulge in the muslin flouncing and this bulge had now disappeared.

I had left nothing of interest or value inside the drawer, so paused only to pull it out by the regulation distance before casting an appraising eye round the rest of the room and the first thing the eye lighted on was my bag, which was on top of the chest of drawers. A quick examination of the contents, followed by a more thorough and pessimistic one, which involved tipping them all out on to the bed, revealed that the only thing to have been removed was the sheet of writing paper to which I had so laboriously committed Nannie's dying words.

Several emotions competed for supremacy, among them anger and outrage, shot through by the first little thread of fear, but there was no time to indulge them and as soon as the initial shock had faded I forced myself to concentrate on practicalities, leading almost immediately to a quick sprint to the writing desk. The pad and envelopes were inside the blotter, just as I had last seen them and I spared a moment to pass a quick vote of thanks to the inventor of the ball-point pen. The impression of my writing on the top page was clear as a bell and there were fainter traces on the second and third as well, so for good measure I tore off the first half dozen sheets and folded them into an envelope which I stuffed inside my bag.

After that I left the room, only to recapture another memory which sent me hurtling inside again. Since it is bad luck to re-enter a room for this purpose without sitting down on the nearest chair and keeping the feet raised off the ground while counting to eleven, I had to spend another few seconds over this ritual before collecting my jacket from the wardrobe. I then left the room again and descended at a leisurely pace to the hall, where Lindy was waiting for me.

'You won't need that, will you?' she asked, eyeing the bag which was now slung over my left shoulder.

'You never know,' I replied. 'All sorts of emergencies could arise.'

'What kind of emergencies?' she asked, looking faintly apprehensive.

'Well, for instance, this may turn out to be quite a stiff ordeal for one of your nervous temperament. You might fall down and bruise yourself, or foam at the mouth. It is as well to be prepared for everything and I always carry a load of first aid equipment in this bag.'

If she were the culprit, it was scarcely to be hoped that she would fall for such a crude trick as that, and I was not specially cast down when she burst into trills of laughter and affectionately linked her arm in my unencumbered one.

'Oh, Tessa, I really do love you! You know why?'

'Not the foggiest.'

'Because you're so different from anyone I ever met before. So mundane, I guess you could call it. And I never know whether to take you seriously, or whether you're just kidding.'

I considered that the same could be said of her, but the heavy bag bumping against my ribs was a constant reminder that someone in the vicinity was up to some pretty sharp tricks and I thought it wiser to stay mundane and appear to take all her remarks at face value.

CHAPTER FIFTEEN

1

THE clump of sycamores known as High Copse was situated on rising ground about half a mile to the east of the main drive, almost in a straight line from West Lodge. To reach it we had first to cross the drive and then to climb the long steep bank on the far side, which eventually brought us out on to open grassland, on a level with the big house and overlooking the lake. Duck-pond would have been a more accurate description of this, but in typically grandiose Chargrove fashion it was always known as the lake. We could see the copse from this point, but the only approach to it was by circling the lake and then climbing up another slope on the far side, all of it in open country.

There were two black cars parked near the stable block and I grabbed Lindy's hand and dragged her, squealing and protesting, back behind a high screen of rhododendrons.

'What's the matter?' she squeaked in great alarm. 'Where are you going, Tessa? Let go of me, will you?'

'It's all right now,' I said, releasing her hand and dropping down on the grass.

'I don't understand,' she complained, still in a high-pitched, tremulous voice. 'What got into you, Tessa?'

'I was trying to save you some embarrassment. Those were police cars down there.'

'So what? They wouldn't have opened fire on us, would they?'

'Probably not. I daresay they weren't even looking in this direction, but if they had caught sight of us it could have been awkward.'

'Why? They couldn't have guessed where we were making for and anyway it's no crime, is it?'

'No, but it occurred to me that if you're too ill to give them a statement about your movements on Saturday night, then strictly speaking you ought to be too ill to go prancing around the countryside.'

'Gosh yes, you're right, I guess,' she admitted, relaxing sufficiently to sit down and select a nice fat stem of grass to chew on.

An odd thing about Lindy was that she invariably had something in her mouth. She was forever biting her thumb knuckle, chewing up blades of grass or, as a last resort, nibbling the ends of her own hair. Perhaps she had cultivated the habit, as visual proof of her immaturity.

'Only thing is, Tessa, I'm not sick in that way. Dr Soames said it would be okay to get up and lead a normal life, only I shouldn't be pressurised in any way, on account of . . .'

'Your psychotic neuroses and tendency to mental instability?' I suggested.

'Right!' she agreed proudly, evidently assured that this time I was not kidding.

'Try telling that to Superintendent Hobley-Johnson.'

'Yeah, see what you mean. I guess your police aren't that wonderful. Well, thanks anyway, Tessa.'

'Don't bother. The evasive action wasn't solely for your sake.'

'No? Whose then?'

'Serena's mainly. She's got enough worries without the police turning all suspicious and fidgety.'

'You wouldn't say they were already?'

'Not seriously, no. They have to go through the motions of carrying out an investigation in accordance with the verdict, but, judging by my own experience, they're being fairly perfunctory and kid glove about it. It looks as though they feel the Coroner was a little over-zealous and that it genuinely was an accident. Either that, or else . . .'

'Else what?'

'They realise that her death was hastened somewhat, as no doubt happens with dozens of senile citizens dotted around the neighbourhood and that they have about as much chance of proving it as you or I would have, if not less. Either way, our best bet is to lie low, be on our best behaviour and not give them any cause to change their policy.'

'So why are they still hanging around?'

'Well, as I told you, they're obliged to dash about a bit and let justice be seen to be having a work out. They've probably gone to interview Primrose, and Mrs Thorne is not far away. She lives in one of the cottages behind the stables. There's Jake too, come to that. He was in the house that evening, though I don't suppose he could tell them any more than that one fact, always assuming that they were still awake when he had done so.'

'Wouldn't bank on that,' Lindy said, chewing away in a ruminative fashion.

'No, only kidding that time.'

'I didn't mean that. I meant about him not having anything he could tell them if he wanted to. I go along with you one hundred per cent that it was accidental, it has to be, but you know something?'

'What?'

'If it weren't an accident, let's just call this thinking aloud, and if it weren't an accident, my money would be on Jake as the killer.'

'What an extraordinary notion! How on earth did you come by it?'

'Oh, I don't know . . . just something I . . . Remember my telling you how I spent that weekend out at Santa Barbara, where I first met Pelham?'

'Vividly.'

'Well, it's a place on the coast, not too far from L.A. and lots of movie people have their homes there, Jake for one, and you get to hear the gossip. Did you know his last wife died of an overdose?'

'I had heard something to that effect; no details though. Is Jake supposed to have killed her? Go on, you may as well tell me the whole bit now you've started.'

'Well, let's just say he didn't work too hard at keeping her alive.'

'I don't call that very conclusive.'

She selected a fresh blade of grass, sucked away at it in silence for a moment or two and then, evidently coming to a decision, said:

'She was a lush and a nympho and the story goes he was fed up to here. Anyway, it wasn't long after she died that he said goodbye to Hollywood and came over to England. He gave it out that he'd made every picture he ever wanted to and as much money as he could ever use, but there could have been a different reason why he needed to leave in a hurry. Maybe the rumours were getting too hot for the Studios to want to go on hiring him.'

'Even so, why come all this way just to repeat the experiment on an elderly female he'd never clapped eyes on before?'

'How about if she'd heard this story about him from Pelham and was going to put it around, so as Primrose wouldn't marry him? No, I'm the one who's kidding now. I know darn well it was an accident, just like you said. And Pelham has the same idea. He agrees with you that the police have to put on an act of being concerned, but they have more important things to do than work themselves into the ground over the death of some poor old invalid woman.'

As it happened, this was not a very accurate paraphrase, but there was a second anomaly which engrossed me still more deeply as, talking of other matters now, we ambled back to West Lodge. If her remarks had truly reflected Pelham's opinion, why had she set out gratuitously to present me with such a lurid version of Jake's marital past?

2

Making fatigue the excuse, I retired to the apricot box soon after dinner, for the necessity of humping the heavy great bag from room to room was becoming excessively tedious and I no longer trusted it out of my sight. Moreover, I had hopes that my departure might fulfil what was becoming a long felt want, in enabling Pelham and Lindy to discuss their plans with Serena, which they had evidently been unwilling to do in my presence. Not a word had been spoken on the subject either before or during dinner and I could tell by the expectant look Serena turned on him every time Pelham opened his mouth that she was still in the dark.

Another incentive was that Primrose was spending the evening with Jake, giving me a clear field to carry out one small but exacting task.

This began with removing the sheets of airmail paper from my bag and inking over the dented impressions. The result was legible, but rather wobbly, so I made a fresh copy, tore the original into a million shreds, enclosed the copy in a covering note and put it into an envelope addressed to Robin.

The nearest pillar-box was two miles away, but there was a system in force whereby the postman on the morning delivery collected outgoing mail from a box beside the front door. I was about to creep down and put my letter inside it when the telephone rang.

I heard Serena answering, after which there was a brief interval, followed by Pelham's voice.

At this point I retreated back into my room, for it had struck me as not inconceivable that were Pelham to notice me going out of the front door with a letter in my hand his curiosity would be aroused to the pitch of being tempted to retrieve it and glance through the contents. Taking no chance of such an eventuality, either then or later, I pushed the envelope under my pillow, picked out a new thriller from the bookcase and lay down on my bed to while away the time until the coast should be crystal clear.

After an hour had passed I was almost as sleepy as I had pretended to be earlier, but still no lights had been switched off and no one had come upstairs. The most frustrating part of all was that having wasted so much time I could no longer depend on myself to waken early enough to catch the postman in the morning. One solution was to try the reviving effects of a hot bath, which involved transferring the letter to my sponge bag, but I had not even got as far as putting one toe in the water when I heard footsteps outside, immediately followed by someone turning the handle and then rapping on the bathroom door. This called for an abrupt change of tactics and, having flung on my dressing gown, I draped a towel round my neck and sauntered on to the landing in the relaxed style of one who had been wallowing inside for hours.

Unfortunately, it was a complete waste of my art, for there was no one in sight and both bedroom doors were shut. I stood beside one of them, announcing in a loud voice that the bathroom was now clear and, receiving no response, opened the door and looked inside.

She was sitting on the bed, not having started to undress and one look was enough to tell me that disaster had struck again. The one I got in return brought the news that, in some inexplicable fashion, it was all my fault.

'Bathroom's okay now,' I said hesitantly.

'No more practical jokes, I trust, Tessa?' she asked, staring at me with stony dislike. 'You wouldn't have left a live toad in the bath, for instance?'

I was so stupefied by this reception that for once I was rendered speechless and she stood up and turned her back on me. I heard her say:

'I don't know what I've done to deserve such treatment, from you of all people, but please leave me alone now and go to bed.'

It was not a tone to admit any argument and I obeyed, closing the door behind me and trudging up to the box room, wondering whether everyone had gone mad, or whether I was on my own.

There was still the letter to dispose of, but I had the whole night for that, since, needless to say, all desire for sleep had now left me.

3

The air had cleared by the morning, although Serena still looked haggard and miserable when I came upon her in the kitchen, where I had gone in search of coffee. She was reading the post, which I was in a position to know had been delivered about ten minutes earlier, but she pushed it aside when I wandered in and, after apologising for speaking so harshly the night before, invited me to sit down while she went to work with the orange juice and coffee grinder. Primrose, it appeared, had already gone out, having breakfasted on a hunk of bread and dripping. Impending nuptials had not so far done much to modify her manners and customs.

'I ought to have known you would never behave so maliciously,' she said, setting the glass down in front of me.

'The trouble is that I speak in haste and regret at leisure, or would if I had any leisure. Last night I felt so distracted after they'd told me the news that I lashed out at the first person who came along and it happened to be you. I am sorry. Do you forgive me?'

'Oh, certainly. What news was that?'

'Because in my heart I know only too well that you're on my side,' she went on, choosing to unburden herself at her own pace. 'You wouldn't have set out to raise false hopes deliberately.'

'Is that what I did?'

'Yes, and you must understand that it was the shock and disappointment which made me so cross. I've got over it now.'

'Got over what?'

'In fact, I regretted it immediately. I lay awake half the night worrying about it, along with all the other horrid things that have happened. At one moment I thought I heard someone creeping past my door and I made sure it was you and that you'd packed your bags and were leaving. Ridiculous, really, because how on earth could you have carried them all the way to the station in the dead of night? Anyway, there are no trains.'

'Yes, it would have been rather madcap.'

'But you know how exaggerated one's fears become in the small hours? In the end I forced myself to go up and make sure you were still there, which of course you were. I could hear you turning over in bed.'

'I wish you'd come in and told me all this at the time.'

'Oh no, darling, you can't imagine that even I would be so selfish as to wake you up just for my own peace of mind?'

'In the first place, I probably wasn't asleep, and if we'd hammered away at it all through the night we might conceivably have got to the nub before dawn broke. I think you mentioned that Pelham and Lindy had some news for you? I suppose you wouldn't care to tell me what it was?'

She brought the coffee and toast over from the stove and sat down at the table, saying with a sigh:

'Yes, I keep forgetting that you don't know yet. Well, brace yourself because Lindy is expecting a baby.'

'So it's out at last! I can't tell you why, but now that it is I find it something of an anti-climax.'

'You won't when you've grasped all the implications.'

'Then I rely on you to tell me what they are, but in the meantime did I dream it or did you tell me when I first arrived that Lindy couldn't have children?'

'No, it's true. At least, it wasn't true, but it was what they told me. Not meaning to deceive, you know, there's no question of that, it was all a misunderstanding. Naturally, I assumed there was some physical reason to prevent it. Wouldn't you have done the same?'

I nodded and she said: 'Well, it wasn't that at all. It was purely a matter of temperament.'

'I don't follow you.'

'No, it is rather incredible, but apparently it stems from something which happened when she was a schoolgirl. Only about sixteen, I gather, and she became pregnant. The boy was only a year older and between them they fixed up an abortion. It had to be done on the cheap because her parents were the old fashioned, puritan sort and she didn't dare ask them for help. The result was that she nearly died of a haemorrhage.'

'I can see how that might put one off, but now that she's respectably married there's no earthly reason to suppose that it could be repeated.'

'Well wait, because that wasn't the whole story. In addition to being at death's door and so on, the experience affected her mind and she went right off the rails for a time. The mere mention of sex gave her the horrors and that was when she took up with this analyst. For two years she visited him every single week and from the way she describes these consultations it sounds rather like going to confessional.'

'And was she finally absolved?'

'Only partially, it seems. What she rather endearingly calls the priority disturbance, the sex phobia, was resolved, as I am happy to say we can all see for ourselves, but she still has to rely on psychiatric treatment and drugs when she feels a fit of hysteria or depression coming on. It seems that these drugs make her very forgetful sometimes, which can lead to embarrassment and, to be candid, Tessa, I can't really see that the game is worth the candle because when they left on this trip she was no nearer being reconciled to the idea of having a baby.'

'So why has she now changed her mind?'

'Extraordinary the power these people have over their patients, isn't it?' Serena asked, pursuing her own train of thought. 'You'll never credit this, Tessa, but apparently he told her that this particular mental block had gone too deep ever to be dislodged and that she must accept it; learn to live with it, to use her own phrase. He said her only hope, if she wanted to live a near normal life was to marry a man older than herself and to establish from the outset that she could never have children; that to do so would almost certainly endanger her sanity. Don't you find that incredible?'

'Not totally, no.'

'Neither did Pelham, as far as I can make out. He married her on those terms and that was that.'

'Only it wasn't, because here they are and everything has changed. Did Pelham break his promise and talk her round?'

'Oh, dear me, no, nothing like that. He was quite prepared to stick to their bargain and they took all the proper precautions. However, it seems that something went wrong once before and when she found she was pregnant they bundled her straight into a clinic. Now it has happened again and she is willing to go through with it, and who do you suppose is responsible for that?'

'Can't imagine. Not me, and not Primrose, presumably?'

'Oh, good gracious no, not Primrose. She doesn't know anything about it yet and I quite dread telling her. The heavens will fall in, I shouldn't wonder, and make a good deal of noise while they do it. No, this is Richard's work. Our own dear Richard Soames! So that makes two things we have to thank him for. There won't be much left of our lives soon, if he keeps it up at this rate.'

'Did he suspect she was pregnant right from the start?'

'No, when she had her first bilious attack he was inclined to put it down to food poisoning. It was that, combined with one or two features about Nannie's death, which made him decide on a post mortem, and we all know what that led to. It wasn't until he saw Lindy for the second time that he put two and two together and told her what he thought was the matter. She immediately flew into the most dreadful panic, but he impressed upon her that the only way to conquer her fears was to go out and meet them, instead of running away.'

'And he won her over, just like that, at the drop of his flat tweed cap?'

'Oh, goodness knows what arguments he used, but he's a clever old monkey and, mind you, Tessa, I don't see what else he could have done. It must have been as plain to him as it is to me that subconsciously she really longs to have a child. Everything is made so easy for you young ones nowadays that it defies belief that this could have happened to her twice in one year, purely by accident.'

'Did they tell you all this last night? No wonder you were so late coming to bed.'

'It didn't take very long, once they got started. It was breaking the ice which was the difficult part. I thought it was so tactful of you to leave us alone, but it didn't work out at all well at first. They sat about patting and pawing each other, you know how they do? Even yawning occasionally, but at the same time you could see they were keyed up, like people are when they're sharing a secret. Then the telephone rang and it was Richard, asking for Pelham. When he came back he smiled at Lindy and gave her the thumbs up sign and that was when the whole story came out. Richard's call was to let them know that the pregnancy test was positive.'

'Whereupon Lindy clapped her hands and cried: "Oh, what a silly girl I've been, but kind Uncle Richard has made everything all right!"?'

'No, not quite. It was really Pelham who was the more elated of the two. All the same, I'm sure that subconsciously it's what she's wanted all along and if she can only keep out of the psychiatrist's clutches it will all work out very well for her.'

'Either that or . . .'

'What?'

'Or they knew about this when they arrived here, but couldn't make it public until . . .'

'Until the doctors had confirmed it? Is that what you were going to say?'

It wasn't, of course, but the alternative explanation which had occurred to me was in too nebulous a form to be shared with anyone else at that stage and, taking my silence for agreement, she said:

'Well, it's possible, but I think you're making everything unnecessarily complicated, as usual. I am sure they would have dropped a hint if that had been the case, and even more sure that they wouldn't have been so set against coming to live here.'

'You mean they've changed their minds about that too?'

'Pelham certainly has. Why else would I be so bothered? It will alter everything for us, and most of all for Primrose just when she was on the brink of achieving her heart's desire. Pelham is convinced the child will be a boy, if not twin boys, and even if he's wrong there's no reason now why they shouldn't try again.'

'Yes, I see. That does make rather a pickle of things.'

'It's not that I mind for myself. In some ways, I'm in favour of the family coming back to Chargrove and it will be nice to have children about the place again. I am sure I shall be able to go on living here, more or less on the same terms as before, but can you imagine what it will do to Primrose?'

'And you say she doesn't know yet?'

'No, not a whisper and I rely on you not to breathe a word. I begged Pelham to leave it to me to find the right moment and he was only too happy to agree. Fortunately, there's no hurry. They'll be going back to the States quite soon and I think it will make it a tiny bit easier if they're not actually on the spot.'

'So they don't plan to move in right away?'

'Oh no, Jake still has a year of his lease to run and they can't force him out if he doesn't wish to go. Pelham talks about wanting the child to be born in this country, so I presume they'll come over a month or two before it's due and take a flat in London until the house is ready for them. It gives one a small breathing space.'

'Furthermore, I'd give you even money that Lindy will talk him out of the whole scheme, once they're back in America. From the way she spoke to me about the prospect of living at Chargrove I would expect her to put up quite a fight.'

'Yes, maybe, but we can't rely on that and what I must put my mind to now is finding some diplomatic way to prepare Primrose for the worst. Any contribution towards that end will be gratefully received.'

CHAPTER SIXTEEN

THE change in Lindy was immediately apparent. It was not that she grew up overnight, for her new fantasy life revealed just the same fundamental immaturity as the old one, but in this short space of time she developed from the child sprite to the child madonna, no longer prancing about with trills and gurgles, but moving among us with sad sweet smiles, in an aura of solemn tranquillity. She did not now perch on the floor, hugging her knees in the Peter Pan style, but sat demurely in the most comfortable armchair, a footstool at her feet and hands folded over a stomach which was still in the concave form, gravely accepting all the little attentions we bestowed on her. It was a good job Primrose was not present, having gone with Jake to an agricultural show in Warwickshire, or it might have penetrated even her miniature brain that something was afoot, and Robin, meeting Lindy for the first time, appeared quite awestruck.

'There was nothing particularly immaculate about that conception,' I reminded him, as we walked out into the park after tea on Friday.

'No, I gather.'

'And she's only in her second month. It's a bit soon to be playing the suffering heroine, wouldn't you say?'

'I do believe you're jealous, Tessa!'

'Me? Jealous of Lindy having a baby?'

'No, jealous of Lindy snatching the star part from under your nose.'

This remark being irrelevant, as well as untrue, I rapidly switched to another topic, asking whether he had received my letter. Most annoyingly, he had not, so I had to give him a verbal report on that and on the circumstances that had led to my writing it.

'Why didn't you tell me this before?' he asked when I had finished. 'That you had recorded Nannie's last words, I mean, and thought they might be significant?'

'But I didn't think so, Robin, that's the whole point. Writing them down was purely a kind of instinctive reflex, but they seemed quite meaningless when I read them the next day. It's only the fact that someone has now gone to the trouble of rifling my bag and removing that one item that makes me realise that it must be important in some way.'

'Well, don't worry. You know what the posts are like nowadays? It will probably be waiting for me when I get back. That is, if you remembered to put a stamp on.'

'Certainly, I did. First class too, which is more than can be said for the other one.'

'Which other one?'

'Oh, there was a letter already in the box when I put mine in. In an airmail envelope.'

'Unstamped?'

'Not enough for America. I nearly went upstairs to get another one to add to it and then I thought: "What the hell? That's one man who can certainly afford to pay at the other end."'

'Why? Was it addressed to a Rockefeller?'

'No, to a doctor in Los Angeles. Lindy's shrink, without a doubt.'

'Well, he won't have to pay a cent because it will be sent by surface mail. You might have thought of that. Too late now though, and in the meantime can you remember exactly what you wrote in yours, or shall we have to wait to find out?'

'No. After writing it out three separate times, I should think you would find it engraved, like Calais, on my heart.'

'Then I suggest that tomorrow morning you write it out once more for my benefit. We'll find an excuse to go for a drive and study it in the privacy of some country lane. Do you suppose it was the reason for your room being searched?'

'Hardly, since no one else knew of its existence.'

'Plenty of people knew that you were the last person to see Nannie alive. They might have suspected you of making some record of the event.'

'That would have been a very lucky shot, don't you think? My theory is that someone may have been looking for her glasses, thinking I had appropriated them, possibly to produce as evidence when the time was ripe.'

'And who, specifically, have you in mind?'

'Oh, they're all equal starters in that race. At least, to be fair, I suppose Primrose is the favourite, since her room is so close to mine and she never needs to account for her presence on the top floor, but any of the others could easily have found an excuse for being up there. Even Jake could have pretended to be looking for Primrose, and Mrs Thorne would only have needed a duster in her hand or the water carafe.'

'Any chance that Mrs Thorne believed the vindictive old nurse to have been responsible for her child's death and decided to get even by sprinkling poison on her porridge?'

'Well, if you put it like that, I suppose there was nothing to stop her, but why wait for nearly twenty years? On the other hand Nannie was in the top bracket of the scandal-monger brigade, who made Mrs Thorne's life such hell after the tragedy, so that could conceivably have festered into a kind of murderous resentment. What's more, she might have had the mistaken idea of doing Serena a good turn by knocking off the old harridan.'

'But you're not convinced that either is a strong enough motive?'

'No, and opportunity is nothing, on its own. There is really no reason why I shouldn't bash you over the head with one of these lumps of wood we keep tripping over, but that doesn't mean I'm going to do it.'

'I am so thankful to hear that. So having eliminated Mrs Thorne, who's your fancy?'

'Oh, Pelham, I suppose. Or maybe Pelham and Lindy as a team.'

'Always assuming he's an impostor?'

'Yes, naturally.'

'Which, if you'll forgive me, I think you assume a little too lightly. It's not all that simple to impersonate a dead man.'

'Nevertheless, I think it could have been done. Let's say that this Pelham, the one we know, is actually John

Smith. He was a friend of the real Pelham and they used to go off to the wilds together, on fishing trips and so on. The real Pelham either dies or is bumped off by J. Smith, who then pinches his passport and other essentials and switches identities. Pelham is a bachelor, with no relatives in America, so it's up to Smith to identify the remains and no reason why anyone in that remote place should doubt him. Any questions?'

'Not on my own behalf, but Smith's relations might want to hear a few more details when they learn of his death.'

'I expect he'd cut loose from them years ago, perhaps when he did his first stint in a British gaol. Because he's an Englishman too, don't forget. That may have been what brought them together in the first place, two expatriates droning on about the Palladium and the Lords' Tavern. John Smith could be an assumed name anyway.'

'Almost bound to be, I should think. So, having acquired a new one, what next?'

'He hops over to New York, joins up with his female accomplice, who has already acquired a passport in the name of Lindy Hargrave, as well as a fictitious background of poor but honest farmers in the Middle West. They then take off on a world trip, proposing to dawdle along in easy stages until the dust has settled. Although it's possible that they have no real intention of ever returning to America; much more likely to pick somewhere like South Africa or Australia, where nothing is known of either John Smith or Pelham Hargrave.'

'Meanwhile, what do they live on?'

'Pelham's money, of course. He's made a packet in real estate, quite apart from the family inheritance, so now his impersonator puts it around that he's married and retired, and the banks in California and London have instructions to remit regular sums to their various foreign branches. I forgot to mention that John Smith had done his first stretch for forgery, but he's become more proficient at it now. Any more questions?'

'Two, but I'll try you with the easier one first. Presumably, the ultimate object of this scheme was to establish himself as lord of Chargrove and either live there in great splendour or turn it to some profitable account, but do you seriously imagine they could get away with it? It's one thing to carry off the sort of bluff you've described, but he'd run into all sorts of legal problems before he could step into Pelham's shoes over here.'

'I'm not sure that it was the ultimate object. I expect they kept it in mind as a possibility, and they came here to spy out the land, but you'll have noticed that from the moment they got the general picture they've disclaimed all intention of settling here. So what had they got to lose? So long as they continued to pass themselves off as visiting relatives, who had popped in to say how do you do, and were never going to make any claim on Chargrove beyond what Pelham had already been receiving ever since Rupert's death, it wouldn't occur to anyone to demand proof of identity.'

'Except Nannie, perhaps?'

'Right, I'm sure John Smith must have heard about her from Pelham during those long chatty evenings in the log cabin, but he couldn't have known for certain whether she was alive, or still had any of her wits about her. I'd guess it came as a sad blow to find the answer was yes to both, because if anyone knew Pelham, warts and all, and was unlikely to be fooled it was she. The only saver was that her sight was failing, so the first move was to pay her a joint visit, in which Lindy was to snatch her glasses while

Smith/Pelham chatted her up. Once this was accomplished it was safe for him to spend hours with her in the nursery, while she did all the talking and he caught up with his own childhood. The big snag was that she wasn't very hot on dates and apt to attribute quite recent events to the distant past and vice versa.'

'Like the death of Alan Thorne?'

'Right. He might have heard about that in a letter, as he afterwards claimed, but he couldn't possibly have known it at first hand. There was another little anecdote too, concerning myself, although neither Serena nor I had any recollection of it. I think he'd seen the danger signals even before the spectacles were found, but that must have put an end to all his schemes because she was a smart old number and once she got a real good look at him the whole game could be up.'

'So Nannie, plus specs, became a danger and had to be removed?'

'With all possible speed. That very night, in fact. It's a good theory, don't you think?'

'Not bad, although I don't see how you reconcile it with the small point that he has now decided to settle at Chargrove. He must see what hazards it will lay him open to. Surely, the sensible course would be to cut his losses and move on?'

'I daresay he will. It would never surprise me if he were to vanish again as soon as the case is officially closed and then write to say he's changed his mind. Meanwhile, since it has now become public that the heir to Chargrove is only seven months away, which may well be the reason why Pelham strove so assiduously to keep Dr Soames away from Lindy's bedside, he may feel that the clever thing would be to appear to modify his attitude to the ancestral home.

Besides, nothing can be put into effect for another year and a lot can happen in that time. He may wish to leave the options open. Was that your last question?'

'No, I have one more, and steady yourself because this is my ace. If you can piece all this together so smoothly, don't you think other people, much more closely involved than yourself, might have had a go too?'

'Oh, sure! Why not?'

'Serena, for one?'

'Yes, Serena, definitely. In fact, although she has never admitted it, I'd say that was her principle reason for inviting me here. I believe she had her suspicions about Pelham from the start. It worried her and she wanted an ally.'

'Then can you explain why she hasn't spoken up? Not a hint of a sign has she given you and furthermore you told me that every time you broached the subject she shied off it and talked of something else. So why? You'd think she'd be only too keen to get your unbiased opinion and, if it coincided with hers, so much the better. If Pelham's a fraud, wouldn't it be to her advantage to make it known?'

'You're so right,' I said thoughtfully. 'Why didn't I think of that before?'

'Even if she'd begun by letting things slide,' Robin went on, rubbing salt in the wound, 'she would certainly take action now that he's threatening to upset things for Primrose.'

'I agree.'

'However tiresome and boring she may find her, I've noticed that she's very protective towards Primrose.'

'Yes, she is. It's partly guilt, I believe. She's always trying to compensate for having neglected her as a baby, because she's convinced that contributed to making her into the creep she is.'

'So the set up is not quite so simple as you'd imagined?'

'Too right.'

'Pity!'

'Are you gloating, by any chance, Robin?'

'On the contrary, I always hate it when your theories fall apart. Frustration doesn't become you. I hoped that by needling you a bit I'd inspire you to find the explanation.'

'Don't worry,' I told him, 'there's one on the way. The trouble is, it's one I'd prefer to be without. I'd better not tell you any more, otherwise you might feel duty bound to follow it up.'

'Although you won't hesitate to do so yourself, I daresay?'

'If only to be proved wrong. Sometimes the best way to blot a thing out is to bring it into the open and look at it from all sides.'

'It can sometimes be quite a good way of getting oneself blotted out too,' Robin reminded me.

CHAPTER SEVENTEEN

THERE was a thump on the door of the apricot box, which could only have been delivered by one powerful fist and, before I could pull myself together, Primrose marched in.

'Saw your light on,' she announced, plumping down on the stool. 'Thought I'd look in and say goodnight.'

'That was very civil of you.'

'No, it wasn't. I'm never civil, as you jolly well know. Can't be bothered. Fact is, I get the creeps up here at night. Keep thinking about . . . well . . . you know . . . can't get used to her not being there any more. Always used to go in for a bit of a natter before I went to bed.'

'She was pretty old, you know. She'd probably have dropped off the hook anyway, in a year or two.'

'Oh, don't give me all that drivel. I'm fed up with it. People ought to know it doesn't make it any better.'

'Did you go in and talk to her on the night she died?'

'You know damn well I did, I told you so. Why?'

'I just wondered if she'd said anything special. Something which might have given a clue to what was on her mind and so on.'

'Yes, of course she did, she went on and on about how ill she felt and, like a clot, I didn't take it seriously. I've told you already, if anyone's to blame it's me.'

'Oh, stop it, Primrose! You can't still be on that dreary old tack? It's such rot.'

'It bloody well isn't, then. Can't you understand? If only I'd got hold of Richard . . . no, maybe not him . . . but . . .'

'Why not Richard?'

'I just wouldn't have, that's all, so mind you own b. I'd probably have got an ambulance and had her bunged straight into the hospital, where they'd have known how to bring her round. 'Stead of that, I just thought she was putting it on, to try and stop me going out.'

'Why would she have been so keen to do that? It was a warm night and not all that late. Besides, you told me that you had a very pressing mission to perform?'

'Oh, that wouldn't have cut any ice with Nan. She didn't really want to stop me doing things, but she couldn't get it through her head that I was grown up. She still expected me to be in bed by nine o'clock with an apple and a cup of Ovaltine. Not that I minded particularly. At least it showed she cared, which was a damn sight more than anyone else did.'

'Remove that mask of tragedy, Primrose, it doesn't suit you. Any fool can see that your mother cares about you tremendously.'

'Oh, baloney! You must be a frightful nit if you can't see through that act. My mother's always loathed the sight of me. She hated me when I was born because I wasn't a boy, and then if I had to be a girl she'd have liked me to be the same sort as her, all frilly and feminine, instead of like my father. I mean, imagine calling me Primrose, for a start!'

'I can't see why that denotes ill will on her part. It's quite a pretty name.'

'I bet you'd never have chosen it for me though, and neither would I. I think it's the most grotty name anyone could be stuck with. Anyway, Nan didn't care a hoot what sex I was, or whether I was ugly or pretty or anything else. She loved me at first because I belonged to my father and then she just loved me for myself.'

'And was it she who filled you up with all those silly tales about your mother?'

'They aren't silly tales. That just shows what a fat lot you know about it!'

'Anyway, the sun will soon shine for you again, won't it, Primrose? You'll have Jake to tuck you up at nine o'clock with your Ovaltine now.'

'Ha ha! Very funny, I must say!'

'Seriously, though, isn't that partly why you're marrying him? Because you terribly need someone to baby you again and love you for yourself?'

'Partly that, I 'spec,' she admitted with one of her sheepish grins, 'but that's not all of it.'

'What else?'

'You really want to know?'

'I think I can guess.'

'Bet you can't then. It's partly to spite Mum. There now, aren't you shocked?'

'Not particularly. I just don't happen to see it as a very solid foundation for a happy marriage.'

'You'd be surprised! I'll get a lot of fun out of it. She's done her best to ruin my life, so I'll have a bash at mucking things up for her, and see how she likes it.'

'Leaving aside your charming filial sentiments, do you imply that your mother seriously considered marrying Jake herself?'

Having, despite my stern efforts not to give her the satisfaction of losing my sang froid, been somewhat stunned by her remarks, it was a pleasure to find that it was now my turn to rock the boat, for her mouth fell open and she stared at me in blank astonishment. Then, breaking into hearty laughter, she spluttered:

'Lord, no. What a silly, footling idea! It wasn't Jake she had her eye on. Someone quite different.'

'In that case, what's to stop her? How does your marrying Jake affect the situation?'

'Lots of ways. First of all, she won't be needed to stick her oar in at Chargrove any more, will she? Everyone thinks I'm a fool, but they'll soon find out that I'm perfectly capable of running the place on my own. I suppose she can go on living here as long as Uncle Pelham lets her, but there won't be all that money floating around from now on.'

'I hardly see that it matters, since you tell me she's planning to marry again.'

'Ah, but perhaps he won't be so keen when she's no longer rich and important. Can't you honestly guess who I'm talking about?'

'There's no reason why I should. I haven't met all Serena's friends.'

She broke into more giggles: 'You've met this one all right, and if you ask me he's begun to cool off already, otherwise he wouldn't have gummed up the works like he did. There now! That's the last clue you're going to get, so you'll have to work it out yourself. Time to hit the hay now. I've got to be up and away by the crack tomorrow. Nighty night, and sleep tight!'

'Nighty night,' I replied in dulcet tones, 'and I hope your Ovaltine chokes you.'

CHAPTER EIGHTEEN

'WE THOUGHT of going for a tour round the countryside this morning, Serena. Is there anything in the cultural line that we ought to look at?'

'Depends how far you want to go. There's a dear little church at Ledbridge, which is only nine miles away.'

'And a dear little pub for Robin? We plan to have lunch out as well. Save you a bit of toil.'

'The Coach and Horses is supposed to be quite good.'

'Any shopping we could do for you, while we're at it?'

'That's very thoughtful of you, darling, and it would save me going down to the village. We need some more steak for dinner. Pelham says Lindy must have lots of protein and they don't seem to feel that any other kind of food would serve the purpose. Thank goodness they'll be leaving tomorrow and we can go back to a normal diet. I never want to see another steak as long as I live.'

'Anything else you need?'

'Just one or two oddments. I'll write them down for you, shall I?'

'Yes, do. I'll probably forget to take the list with me, but no matter. Once read, it will be engraved on my heart for all time.'

I got a sharp look in response to this, but she did not comment and I said, as she handed me the list: 'Tell me, Serena, just suppose for the sake of argument that while they were in London Pelham was run over by a bus, what would become of Chargrove then?'

'Oh, my dearest girl, don't say such terrible things, even in fun. We'd have to go through the whole dreary business all over again, waiting for seven months to see if Lindy had a son.'

'And if it was a girl?'

'Oh, haven't I told you? In that event it would pass to Rupert's uncle; his father's younger brother. He must be very old now, but still alive, as far as I know.'

'And when he died, what then?'

'Well, his son would get it, of course. Who else?'

'You mean old dodderer actually has a son to inherit?'

'Certainly.'

'You flabbergast me!'

'I can't imagine why, Tessa. I've told you often enough of the absurd way Rupert's grandfather disposed of everything. It's been at the root of most of our troubles. I suppose that with two hale and hearty grandsons to leave behind him, he never envisaged any complications, but people should be more careful about playing God when it's going to affect unborn generations.'

'Yes, I understand all that. What rocked me was learning of all these other male heirs cluttering up the script. I don't know why, but I always assumed that the old clergyman was a bachelor.'

'I don't know why either. There's no rule about celibacy in the Church of England, and I don't suppose he has been doddery all his life. Besides, what difference does it make?'

'Only that I'd assumed that after Pelham's death, providing he had no son, the entail could be broken and the estate pass to Primrose and her children.'

'No, nothing of the kind. And now that Pelham has overturned everything by taking on this young wife, the question could only be of academic interest. I'm sure he has a good few years to go before he reaches the doddery stage, and I trust that his chances of being run over by a bus are fairly remote. Now, hadn't you better make a start, if you mean to see anything before lunch?'

As Robin had pointed out, bringing things into the open does not always have the desired effect, but at least I had advanced another step forward, albeit one which led in the wrong direction.

CHAPTER NINETEEN

1

'I CAN only assume she was referring to Richard Soames,' I explained, answering Robin's question as we drove through the main gate and turned right for Ledbridge. It was the first opportunity we had had for a private conference since the previous evening and I was bringing him up to date in chronological order, beginning with my late night chat with Primrose.

'I must confess,' I went on, 'that I don't know whether to believe it or not. Serena's always been so stuck on this idea of not marrying again.'

'You think Primrose might have invented it? But why? And why take you into her confidence? I never thought you two were on particularly chummy terms?'

'Neither did I, but I think that part was probably true. She really does miss her old Nan and the cosy times they used to have of an evening. I just happened to fill the breach last night and that's what worries me. With all her faults, no one has ever suggested she was a liar.'

'On the other hand, her view of life is faintly distorted, isn't it? Specially where her mother is concerned.'

'Yes, you're right and it's most likely a case of self-delusion, rather than direct lying. Serena told me once that there was an idea floating around that Primrose might marry Richard herself, but it fizzled out. Probably he was the one to hang back, but because of this obsession she has about her mother hating her, she's persuaded herself that Serena warned him off out of jealousy.'

'More likely still, had allowed the old nurse to persuade her.'

'Right again! That's far more logical, but unfortunately it adds another brick to the growing pile and what I need is a brisk wind to come along and blow it all down. Why are we stopping? I don't see any church.'

'No, but we'll be far enough off the road under this tree and I think it's time to have a squint at our victim's last words. You never know what breeze they may stir up.'

I took a sheet of paper from my bag on which Nannie's last message had been recorded for the fourth time and began to read it aloud in a flat, expressionless voice, as though it were a telegram: 'No. no time, help me. should have told them, tell Mummie not her fault, not my baby, should have. boy. not the other one. should, sorry Mummie.'

About forty minutes later, when we had re-read it a dozen times, chopped it into sentences, tried out countless conflicting interpretations of each, and done just about everything except translate it into Chinese, Robin said:

'All right then, if we postulate a conspiracy of silence, with murder at the centre of it, how many other people, apart from those we've mentioned, would you say were involved?'

'Three certainly; probably four and possibly five.'

'Including the two Thornes?'

'I'm not sure about Ted, but it wouldn't surprise me. After all, if our reconstruction is correct, he wouldn't have had any special affection for the child and Alice, being a pious type, probably saw it as just retribution.'

'Even so, would they really have kept quiet about a thing like that?'

'When you consider their built-in feudal attitudes and who they were protecting, I should say they probably would have. To put it on a slightly lower level, they had no proof and, to reduce it to the lowest level of all, good jobs in agriculture, with free houses and unlimited produce thrown in, weren't all that easy to come by.'

'How about the doctor?'

'May have guessed, don't you think? It would account for a lot and he must already have been in practice by then.'

'Though for a man in his position wouldn't it have been a positive duty to take some action, however vague the evidence?'

'Oh, love is a great conscience quietener.'

'You hope!'

'Well, when you think of the times you've covered up for me, against your better judgement.'

'And do you think he was in love with her all those years ago?'

'Of course I do.'

'Then why, having kept quiet for so long, did he go out of his way to publicise the fact that there was something fishy about the old woman's death? It was from his testimony that the verdict followed.'

I know, and I've been wondering about that too. It was odd, but l think I can explain it, to myself at least.'

'Then try and do the same for me.'

'I think he must have got in too deep to pull himself out when he realised where it was leading. Something about Nannie's death may have struck him as inconsistent with her case history and that, combined with Lindy's attack, could have given him the idea of food poisoning. At this point, of course, no thought of murder would have entered his head, but he would have felt an obligation to verify the suspicion and, if necessary, trace the source of the poison. That's how any medical mind would operate, isn't it?'

'And so?'

'So, having failed for one reason and another to obtain any specimens for analysis, he has no choice but to carry out a post mortem. Unfortunately, he didn't warn anyone of this intention until he was committed to it and when the results became known there was no drawing back. Other people had been involved in the autopsy and when he went into the witness box he had to tell the truth. It's ironic, really, because if Lindy hadn't been starting a baby none of it would have happened.'

'Incidentally, I was under the impression that it was morning sickness that women in her condition suffered from. Nobody said anything about midnight sickness.'

'I believe it can creep up on you at any old time and in any case you wouldn't expect Lindy to have just the normal symptoms, would you? It would be a point of honour with her to jiggle them around a bit. Also, to be fair, she may have guessed she was pregnant and part of the nausea came from sheer fright, or even that she'd got a hint of what was going on and was scared on that account.'

'Nothing would surprise me about that pair,' Robin admitted, starting the engine as he spoke. 'Come on, I need a drink before we go into battle. What's the name of this place we're supposed to be making for?'

'Ledbridge. It's just down the road, and fear not! I've already checked up on the amenities and we're recommended to the Coach and Horses.'

'How about this friend of yours, Hobley-Johnson?' Robin asked, when we had found our way to the bar.

'He seems quite harmless.'

'Local boy, would you say?'

'Could easily be. Why?'

'Old enough to have been on that case?'

'I shouldn't think he'd have much recollection of it, and surely the file will have been closed years ago?'

'Then they can open it up again. You never know, there might be statements from witnesses which would give us a lead, maybe even a photograph or two.'

'You do realise, Robin, that it could have been Rupert all the time and not Pelham at all?'

'Oh yes,' he replied cheerfully, 'I should say that's more than likely.'

2

The Superintendent was not at his headquarters and was not expected back for several hours. Robin who was not prepared to give anything away at this stage, least of all his identity, said the matter was not urgent and we should call back later. The desk sergeant received the information with a somewhat old-fashioned look, but did not comment and we repaired once more to the Coach and Horses.

The lunch was not at all bad, the church lived up to Serena's recommendation and the archives of the local newspaper yielded a small harvest, but none of them really warranted the careful attention they got, for, as we afterwards learnt, about half of that time had been spent by the Superintendent on our very own doorstep at West Lodge. It is doubtful, however, if he would have had much of it to spare for us, had we been aware of this, for he had been summoned there to look into the disappearance of Lindy Hargrave.

She had been missing for not much more than an hour when the police were called in, which on the face of it looked a bit like jumping the gun, but there were various factors to account for it. When finally pieced together, the story was as follows:

Immediately after luncheon Lindy had gone upstairs for her prescribed afternoon rest, leaving Serena alone with Pelham, who had shortly become bored and restless and had taken himself off for a walk round his estate.

Grateful for a little solitude for once, Serena had slipped into a doze on the parlour sofa, from which she was awakened at four o'clock by Mrs Thorne, who had brought her some tea. At her request, Mrs Thorne had then taken a tray up to the spare room, returning almost immediately with the news that no one was there.

Pelham was the first to return and he seemed relatively unmoved by his wife's absence. She was not given to solitary excursions, but fresh air and exercise had also been prominent among Dr Soames' recommendations and she was following them meticulously. It was therefore assumed that she had gone for a walk, having left the house very quietly in order not to disturb Serena.

Primrose had arrived home ahead of her usual time, explaining that she had to change into what she called her glad rags, as she and Jake were invited to a cocktail party on the other side of the county. In answer to their enquiries, she said she had come straight from the stables and had not seen anything of Lindy.

In due course Jake had arrived to collect her and they had left the house together about ten minutes later. The small bustle created by these comings and goings had caused Pelham and Serena to lose count of the time and it was not until they were alone again and found that it was past five o'clock that the mood had become tinged with alarm, the reaction, in Pelham's case, being to take a stroll outside and have a look-see.

Alone once more, Serena had attempted to stifle her growing uneasiness by taking up her needlework, but had hardly got going on the first stitch when she was again interrupted by Mrs Thorne, who came bursting into the room brandishing a letter. She had found it on Lindy's dressing table, when she went in to turn down the beds. Having read only two sentences, Serena had leapt up and run into the hall, reaching the front door at the same instant as Pelham entered it. In as few words as possible she had made him see the urgency of the situation and he had picked up the telephone even before she had finished speaking.

We did not see this letter, which had brought matters to a head, until much later, for the Superintendent's first act had been to take possession of it; but in the interval before he arrived, Serena had read it all through and was able to give us a reasonably accurate transcription.

Anything closer could hardly have been expected of her, for it had obviously been composed by a trembling hand and a mind under great stress. Parts of it were illegible, others incomprehensible.

'Like a stream of consciousness,' she told us, 'with no beginning or end, practically no punctuation and allusions to her childhood all mixed up with the present and future. It wasn't clear whether she meant that her mother had tried to kill her, or that she had tried to kill her own child. It was so painful, and poor Pelham is distraught. I never felt so sorry for anyone in my life; but the drift of it was that she felt she was being tricked into having this baby and she simply could not face it. Her great fear, apparently, was that if it were born she might not be able to restrain herself from killing it, and it would be better for everyone if she were to kill herself first. Terribly unbalanced, poor child!'

'But I thought that was all over, Serena? Didn't you tell me the clever old doctor had fixed everything?'

'Yes, I did, but the neurosis must have been far more serious than he or Pelham realised, and I suppose once the novelty had worn off all the old fears came crowding back.'

'So what's the position now?'

'Oh, the search goes on, just like the last time. To think of being asked to live through all that again! Someone said they were going to drag the lake next. Of course there was no need for that last time because it was frozen over, but otherwise it's like some terrible, recurring dream, and as far as I can see it might go on for hours. We shall probably sit here all night, not knowing what's become of her and whether she's alive or dead. I can't bear to think what Pelham must be suffering.'

'Is he out searching as well?'

'Oh yes, not that he had any more notion than the rest of us where she might have got to, but he couldn't just sit here doing nothing. How about you, Robin? You've had more experience than the rest of us, have you any idea where someone in that state of mind might have made for?'

'None whatever, but I'm quite ready to join in the hunt as soon as someone gives me my orders. These operations can only hope to succeed when they're co-ordinated, so there's no point in going off in a haphazard way on my own. Perhaps I should go down to the lake and offer my services to the Superintendent?'

'Wait a minute, Robin,' I called as he moved towards the door. 'Just hang on while I get a coat and I'll come with you.'

'Hadn't you better stop here and look after Serena?'

'Oh no, let Tessa go too, if she thinks she can help. I'd offer to go myself if I didn't know how useless I'd be. It would be more than I could stand.'

'I thought it would be unwise to mention this in front of Serena,' I explained, as we hurried towards the lake, 'but I've a sort of idea where Lindy would have gone, if she'd really intended to do away with herself.'

'Presumably any hunch is worth following up.'

'I think she might be in High Copse. You know, the place where they found Alan Thorne. It had a morbid fascination for her and the setting would have appealed to her sense of drama. Anyway, I think it's far more likely than the lake.'

'So it's worth a try, although personally I feel that the Ophelia role would also have had its attractions.'

'Then you agree with me that this may turn out to be a case of straight exhibitionism?'

'Couldn't say, but there's always a good chance.'

'Yes, and that was another thing it was best not to say in front of Serena. It would be a shame to raise false hopes, but I would never be surprised if this turns out to be one of those scenes where she scares everyone silly and then contrives to get pulled back from suicide in the nick of time. That pathetic farewell letter was pretty prominently displayed.'

'Let's hope you're right.'

'I am full of quiet confidence,' I confessed. 'Not only is she a show-off by nature, but I would have sworn she had become reconciled to motherhood and was revelling in the situation. Well, you saw yourself what she was like yesterday, Robin; radiance zooming out all over her. I can't believe it was all just an act, or that the mood could have changed so drastically in twenty-four hours.'

'Let's hope you're right,' he said for the second time. Unfortunately, repetition did not make it true, although one hunch, at least, had been correct. They found her lying under the spreading branches of a sycamore tree, close by the one where Alan had been tied up and left to die. She had been shot through the head at very close range by a gun which belonged to Pelham and which lay on the ground beside her outstretched hand. The only part of me which remained unshaken by this news was the conviction that she had not been in a suicidal frame of mind.

CHAPTER TWENTY

'WE THINK it's about time you came clean, Serena,' Robin said. 'No need to look scared,' he added, though unfortunately not in time to prevent its happening.

'Is this an official enquiry, Robin?'

'No, on the contrary.'

'Then kindly don't address me as though I were a hostile witness.'

'Is that how I sounded? It was not intentional because I speak as a friend.'

'And what is it you want to know?'

'Nothing.'

'My dear boy, do stop playing ridiculous games.'

'There is nothing I want to know because Tessa and I believe we have worked it out for ourselves. All we want is for you to own up. In my opinion, keeping quiet any longer can do nothing but harm, both to yourself and Primrose.'

The needle, which had been plying relentlessly in and out, now quivered and stopped, but she managed to retain a governessy tone of voice as she asked:

'Is there some connection between these riddles and that poor child's death, by any chance?'

'Which poor child?'

'Lindy, of course. Who else?'

'There may be a link of kinds.'

'Perhaps you can help me, Tessa? I can't seem to get any sense at all out of Robin.'

'I am afraid the trouble is that he is trying to get some sense out of you and all you have done so far is ask questions.'

'Then let me ask another. Is he hinting that . . . that the police are not satisfied that it was suicide?'

'They have not admitted it,' Robin said, answering for himself, 'but I daresay the possibility has passed through their minds, as it must have passed through everyone's. However, they can't build a case on that. It is an odd situation in a way because on the one hand we have a death which will probably go down in the annals as accident, but which meanwhile has been classified as murder, and on the other we have a death in slightly more suspicious circumstances which is likely to be written off as suicide.'

'You really think so?' Serena said, letting out her breath in a long sigh.

'Don't bank on it because I was wrong before, but the signs all point that way. The gun had her prints on it and the letter is authentic, no possibility of forgery. No one can dispute that it showed a mind most seriously disturbed and in fact the American doctor has been contacted and will send written testimony to confirm that she was unbalanced and had attempted suicide at least twice before.'

'So what more proof could anyone need?'

'It's true that attempted suicide is a different matter from the real thing, but I'd say you'll be all right. The trouble is it won't end there. There'll be talk, won't there? Rumour, gossip, people staring at you when you're out shopping, old friends mysteriously dropping off. All the things you dread most, in fact. And the curious part of it is, you know, that none of this would have arisen if it hadn't been for Nannie's death and all the publicity that followed it. One neurotic young woman's suicide would soon have been forgotten in the ordinary way. Coming so quickly after the other it is bound to cause a stir.'

'Oh yes,' Serena replied bitterly, 'I grant you that. It was only to be expected that her malevolent spirit would haunt us for years after she was dead, I've said so all along. Well, I suppose we must grit our teeth and get through as best we can.'

'I think you can do better than that,' Robin told her. 'A little frankness on your part would at least clear the air. For a start, how long is it since you became convinced that Pelham really was Pelham and not, as in Tessa's romantic version, some stranger impersonating him?'

Serena reacted like someone who had been led blindfold to a ditch and then told to jump. She was over it before she had seen what it consisted of.

'Since the night of Nannie's death,' she replied promptly. 'Why? What does that matter?'

'I'll tell you in a minute, but let's get a few other things clear first. Up to that point you'd suspected he was a fraud, is that right?

'Yes.'

'And when did the suspicion start. From the day he and Lindy arrived here?'

'No, not so soon. The idea took hold of me very gradually and I can't tell you exactly when or how it began. Perhaps it was his not wanting me to invite any of his old friends who still live in the neighbourhood; all he asked was to spend every free minute in the nursery, churning over ancient history with Nannie. It seemed so unnatural. Then he would join us for meals and regale us with another stack of reminiscences about his boyhood, and it made me wonder if it was a deliberate policy to get Nannie to burble on, so as to pick up all sorts of knowledge that he ought to possess if he were truly Pelham. Lindy's behaviour rather bore that out. She never appeared to resent his neglecting her; she seemed perfectly content to spend her time with me, a stranger and not even her own nationality or generation. Naturally, I began to think they were in the plot together.'

'So you panicked?'

'No, I didn't, that's much too strong a word. I became a little uneasy, that's all, and worried about what steps I should take.'

'So you sent for Tessa?'

'Yes. I badly wanted someone to talk it over with. Or rather, I thought if Tessa came to the same conclusion, without any prompting, it would give me the backing I needed and that between us we might work out what action to take.'

'However, in between inviting Tessa here and her arriving, you had begun to see the light?'

'What light? I don't understand you.'

'I mean that knowing Tessa was on her way here gave you the confidence to study the problem in a more sober fashion. By the time she arrived you had realised that your best interests depended on Pelham alive rather than dead, and that a spurious Pelham was better than no Pelham at all.'

'Really, Robin, a mind reader as well! That must be a great advantage in your job.'

'No, you flatter me because your actions speak for themselves. How else can one explain your reluctance to discuss Pelham with Tessa? Normally, the pair of you would have spent hours pulling him to shreds and any doubts she had expressed as to his being the genuine article would have made it all the merrier. Yet, whenever she approached within miles of the subject you fobbed her off, or pretended not to hear. The fact was that by then you didn't want it raised, by her or anyone else, but most especially by her, with her awkward police connections. Legal investigations might have followed and, had it turned out that your real brother-in-law was dead, where would that have left you and Primrose? Up the creek, most likely, with a completely strange family at Chargrove, owners of the house you live in and powers to cut off your income overnight, if they chose.'

'If all that is true,' Serena said, 'I don't appear to have been very successful in my duplicity, do I? Since you have seen through it without my saying a word.'

'Ah, but it doesn't matter to you now, does it? You have become much more outspoken about the number of heirs around, alive and kicking to replace Pelham, now that you know he is what he claims to be. It was only when you had doubts that you were a little evasive as to who would inherit. There is one thing you can tell me though, if you will?'

'How very surprising!'

'You said it was on the night of Nannie's death that you decided he was the true Pelham. What in particular happened that evening to make you change your mind?'

'Oh, it was when he brought up the subject of Alan Thorne.'

'Because you knew that was the one topic she would never have discussed with him?'

'So you're not surprised after all? My one poor bubble of triumph has been burst before it even got off the ground.'

'Well, at least you can explain to us why he couldn't have learnt about it from that source.'

Serena looked from one to the other of us, as though turning over the answer, or maybe various alternative answers in her mind and I said:

'I am sure it is my turn to have a small triumph now. Was it because she knew the truth about Alan's birth that the subject was forbidden?'

'What a team you make!' she sighed. 'Quite irresistible when you combine forces. Yes, I am sure she did know, although we never discussed it. It was one reason why she was so jealous and resentful of poor Alice and, for anyone who had known Pelham as a child, the resemblance was unmistakable. I believe a lot of people believed Rupert was the father, which was sheer nonsense, of course, although he did take full responsibility.'

'And that was why you insisted on our calling her Mrs Thorne instead of Alice?'

'Yes, I knew I could rely on her discretion and her sad, difficult life has changed her looks so much that there was small risk of his recognising her. The name Thorne meant nothing to him, you see. He had only known her as Alice.'

'Was that why he went to Canada?'

'Partly, I daresay, though not of course the main reason. You see, this happened at about the time that Rupert and I got engaged and Pelham was bitterly jealous. He simply couldn't tolerate anyone else taking first place with his brother. Then on top of this blow there was the unpleasant fact of having got one of the maids into trouble, as they used to call it. They'd left it far too late for an abortion and anyway I doubt if Alice would have consented to such a thing, with her strict Methodist upbringing. Pelham always lacked moral fibre when it came to the testing point and presumably he thought the simplest way out was to cut loose and leave someone else to clear up the mess.'

'Which Rupert obligingly did?'

'Yes, and in a typically practical, no-nonsense way. He offered Ted Thorne one of the best cottages on the estate, dangled a nice fat cheque, to start him off in married life and had him and Alice at the altar in a matter of weeks. It wasn't altogether a successful match, but that's another story. And really, you know, I do wonder why we are talking about it at all? I can't see what bearing it has on our present troubles.'

'Quite a lot, in my opinion,' Robin said, 'but there is still one thing that puzzles me. If Pelham didn't hear about Alan

Thorne's death from Nannie, who did tell him? He said the news must have come in a letter, but was it from you?'

'No, such a thing never occurred to me. There was absolutely nothing he could do about it and I concluded that he had long ago put the whole episode of Alice out of his mind and would hardly welcome such an unpleasant reminder of it.'

'Could Alice have written herself?'

'No, certainly not. One of Rupert's conditions was that Ted should accept responsibility for the boy and she would never have gone behind his back. Besides, none of us knew his address. Letters could only be sent to him through the lawyers or the bank.'

'All the same, he did hear about it from someone, so who could it have been.'

'If you want my candid opinion, Robin, I think he read it in a newspaper.'

'Oh, surely not? A story like that would hardly rate the *Los Angeles Times*, would it?'

'No, but I remember that most of the London dailies carried a line or two on it and naturally the local papers had a field day. Pelham always had a shifty side to him, you know, not a bit like Rupert in that respect, and it's my belief that he's been in this country at least once during the past twenty years. I actually caught sight of him myself, at any rate I could have sworn it was he, in a taxi which passed me in the Brompton Road. Of course he had a perfect right to come here whenever he chose, I'm not denying that.'

'Only why all the secrecy?'

'Well, that's his way. He always liked to play the lone wolf, but you can easily imagine how, if Alan's death had happened to coincide with one of these visits and he had read something about it in a newspaper, his recollection of the event would have become blurred over the years, so that it merged into all the other Chargrove memories. You have to remember that he had left here before the child was born, so the name wouldn't have made any impact on him, to make the episode stand out.'

'And what was the purpose of these clandestine visits, do you suppose?'

'Pure sentiment, most likely. He'd made a new life for himself in America and a lot of money and no doubt he was enjoying it all hugely. Nevertheless, for an expatriate, he's stayed almost aggressively English and I am sure there were times when he hankered for his native air; but not to get involved in the old life any more, that was never his object.'

'So why has all that changed? Why come here quite openly this time, practically force himself into your household and spend all his time raking over past history?'

'Enough questions, Robin. I shall give you the privilege of answering that one.'

'Perhaps Tessa should do so instead? She has been abnormally silent all this while.'

'A change of heart?' I asked, endeavouring to rise to the occasion. 'Getting married was one indication of that. Perhaps the thrill had gone out of money making and he was ready to pack it in. Naturally, he would be drawn to this country as a possible place to settle down in and so his visit was a form of reconnaissance, a way of breaking down some of the barriers and seeing what lay behind them. Nursery gossip and soaking up the atmosphere of the place wasn't such a bad way of beginning.'

Serena nodded approvingly: 'I agree.'

'Do you?' Robin asked. 'Then why was it that until he knew about the baby he was so insistent that he never meant to stay for more than a week or two?'

'I think we were taken in over that, you know. It was really Lindy's version, not his. She was appalled at the prospect of living here and maintained that she and Pelham thought alike on the subject, but I never saw any evidence of it on his side, did you, Serena? I think he had fallen in love with the place all over again and secretly hoped that as time went by he would convert Lindy to the idea. It was a vain hope, in my opinion, but I doubt if he realised it.'

Serena nodded again: 'Quite so, my dear, I agree with every word. So now that we have thrashed it out and have found that our views coincide, I will ask you once more: what was the purpose of these questions?'

'You have answered that yourself,' Robin told her, 'and I am so relieved to have dragged it out of you, even though it took so long. As we've agreed, there'll be a lot of unpleasant talk about Lindy's death, whatever the official verdict, and some misguided people, including your double barrelled Superintendent, might be under the impression that if any two people stood to gain by it they were you and Primrose. You have now revealed that this is not so and that you were under no illusions as to where your interests lay. In short, Pelham and his heirs were far more valuable to you alive than dead.'

Serena gave careful consideration to this absolution and then said:

'I never expected I should have to defend myself against a charge of murder, still less to set myself up as a candidate for one, but there is something you have overlooked. The situation had changed. He was determined that the child should be brought up here. It must have made a difference.'

'But Tessa doesn't believe that Lindy would have co-operated in that plan, do you, Tess?'

'No. I grant you that a few more bracing talks with Dr Soames might have carried her through to the point where natural maternal instincts took over, though personally I believe that once back in the bosom of her analyst all that would have come unstuck. Whether it did or not, I still can't see her consenting to live at Chargrove. She had a horror of the place, for which I'd be the last to blame her and she'd have been a complete fish out of water. I bet you anything that once they were back in America she'd have worked on Pelham until he dropped the idea. Don't you think I'm right?'

'Who except you would believe me if I said I did? And if they believed it of me, they certainly wouldn't of Primrose. She is not noted for her powers of perception.'

'Primrose knew nothing whatever about the baby. You made us promise not to tell her.'

'One of you could have broken your word.'

'Who? Not either of us. If Pelham or Lindy had done so, which is highly unlikely, it could only have been sometime this morning, and you would certainly have noticed the effect at lunch time. She wouldn't have taken that bit of news in her stride. I can also tell you that she came and sat in my room last night, after the rest of you had gone to bed, and I swear on my oath that she hadn't heard a whisper of it. The whole trend of her conversation was based on her future life at Chargrove. She is not noted for her powers of deception either. Furthermore, you'll recall that she was up and away and out of the house this morning before the others came down. There simply wouldn't have been an opportunity for either of them to have told her.'

'And all this is to come out in a court of law? Is that what you're hinting?'

'Not necessarily,' Robin said. 'Unlikely, in fact, but there is the inquest to be faced and possibly other enquiries as well. I simply wanted you to see for yourself that your best protection is in telling the truth.'

Serena gave us both a long, speculative look before saying quietly:

'Leaving nothing out?'

'That's up to you, isn't it? No point in dragging out past history, unless it happens to be relevant to the present.'

Her look hardened, but she said no more and I could hardly blame her, for at that moment you could have knocked me cold with a bootlace. The last thing I had ever expected to hear was Robin urging a witness to conceal evidence and I could only conclude that it was his method of paying out another inch or two of rope.

CHAPTER TWENTY-ONE

1

IT WAS the same coroner as before and this time he was taking no chances. Having had it spelt out for them, the jury dutifully returned a verdict of suicide while the balance of the mind was disturbed.

Pelham, who, without explanation had removed himself to London two days beforehand, came back for it and was the first witness to be called after the ballistics expert had said his piece. He was given an easy passage and no allusions were made to the folly of leaving loaded firearms around where the possessors of disturbed minds could get at them. Serena was taken through the events leading up to Lindy's disappearance, which she told in the same words as she used to us, and Mrs Thorne described how she had found the suicide note.

The proceedings closed with the court's sympathy being extended to the bereaved family, and Primrose and Jake, who had been sitting a little apart from the rest of us, followed behind in Jake's car to West Lodge, where we all had tea.

Robin had also returned for the occasion and, looked at with a dispassionate eye, it was a macabre little scene; six adult people crowded into Serena's doll's house parlour, being waited on by a seventh and one of them a double murderer.

Afterwards, Jake and Primrose drifted hand in hand back to the stables and Robin declared himself ready to set off to London. However, I told him that I had agreed to stay for one more night. In fact, I was under an obligation to do so, for Pelham was also staying overnight, in order to pack up Lindy's belongings and arrange for them to be shipped to her family in the States, and Serena could not face spending an evening alone with him. Naturally, I did not explain all this in front of the others and, as there was also another small matter I wished to discuss with him in private, I put on a wifely expression and went out to the car to see Robin off.

When I returned, Pelham, who had made a good start on the whisky, said he would be happy to give me a lift to London in the morning. There were various reasons why I did not intend to accept this offer, but as I could find no words to express them inoffensively, I thanked him and allowed the problem to await the inspiration of the morning.

How much of the evening Serena would have been forced to spend alone with him, had I not been there, was also open to question, but in the event he hardly appeared at all, refusing even to come down to dinner, although prudently taking the whisky bottle upstairs to his room.

He and I did not meet again until I had gone up myself and was passing the door of the nursery bathroom as he came out of it.

'What have you been doing in there?' I asked rather thoughtlessly, and also unwisely as it happened, for the question put him into quite a fury:

'Don't you ever stop asking damn silly questions? And has it escaped your vigilant eye, Miss N. Parker, that the plumbing amenities are in very short supply in this matri-archal establishment? The other bathroom happens to be occupied and, being so sharp, you may have noticed that it is blowing a gale outside, as well as pouring with rain.'

The sarcasm was so leaden that I did not attempt to counter it. His lower lip, turned down in its habitual pout, was actually trembling and I reckoned that only a little bait-ing would be enough for him to hit me or burst into tears. However, he did not omit to give my ear a half hearted tweak before he turned away, suggesting that he would not remain inconsolable for ever. On the other hand, he was patently slightly drunk, so perhaps it was a mistake to place too much significance on the gesture.

While I was taking my turn in the bathroom, I heard a slapping, rustling sound from the nursery, followed by a loud click, both of which were repeated several times at irregular intervals. However, I did not allow myself to slide into the grip of mortal terror for more than a second or so, for common sense soon informed me that the noises did not emanate from Nannie's ghost tramping around the nursery, but from the aforementioned elements. Sure enough, when I nerved myself to investigate I found that the dormer window had not been properly secured on its bar and that with each gust of wind that slammed it shut the curtains ceased their merry billowing and flapped back against the panes.

The fact that these sounds had been so clearly audible in the room beyond, combined with a half forgotten observation of Lindy's, and a much more recent one from Pelham, crystallised an idea which had been hovering in my mind for some time and encouraged me to try an experiment. Unfortunately, it was one which needed an accomplice and I did not much fancy either Pelham or Serena in this role. Luckily there was a substitute of sorts close at hand and I went up to the shelf to inspect it. It appeared to be in working order, so the next job was to dig out the pile of old records from the toy cupboard and select the one most suitable for the purpose, which happened to be Bob Newhart's monologue about the driving instructor. I put it on the turntable, set the needle in place and, as soon as the record started, nipped back to the bathroom, taking care to shut both doors behind me.

It was a long time since I had heard that particular sketch and I had forgotten how funny it was. Some of the lines actually forced me to stifle my laughter, but the real reward was that I could hear every word as plainly as though the record was playing in the same room. Ten out of ten to Mr Newhart, and A plus to me, for I now knew beyond all doubt who had committed the murders and why.

Regrettably, however, this complacent mood was soon dashed for on returning to the nursery I found that some-one had arrived there ahead of me. She was standing with her back to the door, bending over the gramophone, whose arm was now slithering about in the centre of the record, and when she turned round I saw that she had a carving knife in her hand.

2

There were doubtless a number of ways in which I could have dealt with the situation, but not for a fraction of a second did I hesitate to take the cowardly one. It was a simple matter of reflex to withdraw to the landing, slam the door shut and bolt for the stairs. Gathering momentum, I sped past Pelham's door, then Serena's, took the second flight at a gallop and had streaked through the hall and out of the front door in thirty seconds flat.

It had stopped raining, but the wind was still blowing fiercely enough to snatch most of my dwindling store of breath and almost knock me off balance. Mercifully, there was only a short distance to go, for Robin's car was parked at the prearranged spot on the main drive and he was sitting inside it, looking excessively bored.

'I thought I told you to stay in your room and lock the door?' he said when I had staggered up to the car and flopped into the passenger seat. 'I'd have seen your light perfectly well if you'd signalled, as we arranged.'

I was still out of breath and had a stitch in my side, so for once he was able to continue uninterrupted, which he proceeded to take advantage of, in a somewhat aggrieved fashion:

'If only you'd stick to the schedule! You gave me a heart attack, leaping out of the darkness like that.'

Still no answer and the novelty of the situation may have begun to pall, for he said crossly:

'You're not hurt or anything, are you?'

'No, just puffed. Getting better though.'

'Okay, take your time.'

'That's just what I can't do, nor you either. We must get back there as fast as we can. She might go berserk.'

I described my experiment and how I had literally been caught in the act and when Robin had gathered up a few items from the back seat we set forth at a brisk trot through the wind and darkness to West Lodge.

'Do you think she grasped what you were up to, Tess?' he asked, as we paused for a breather under the porch.

'May have. She's known me long enough. I daresay she's caught on to how my mind works by now.'

'All the same . . .'

'Yes, I know. She must have armed herself with the knife before she came upstairs and she couldn't have heard the record until she got there, so that can't have been the cause.'

'Which means it was premeditated. In that case, I can't quite see what all the hurry is about. Who else might be in danger? Not Primrose?'

'Oh no, not Primrose. She isn't even here. At least she hadn't come in when I left.'

'Well, that's something. It looks as though we'll have enough problems on our hands without that one. Would you prefer to stop here for a bit, while I go and sort her out?'

'Oh no, I expect she'll have cooled down by now, and I can always cower behind you if it gets rough.'

'Mind your back then!' Robin said, pushing open the front door and walking ahead of me into the hall.

CHAPTER TWENTY-TWO

'I NEVER meant to harm you,' Serena was saying five minutes later. 'I do wish I could make you believe that, though I'm afraid it's impossible.'

We had moved into the kitchen, possibly because all three of us had felt instinctively that the carving knife, now reposing on the table, would look more at home there than among the silks and snuff boxes of the parlour.

'I do believe you, as a matter of fact,' I told her.

'Oh, Tessa, do you really? How wonderful to hear that! You can't imagine the relief, and I can see you mean it. You know that I could never, never have been so wicked. You've always been such a true friend, more like my own daughter.'

'It is all very well for you two, splashing about in your bath of tears,' Robin complained, 'but perhaps one of you could explain to me what Serena was doing in Tessa's room with a dangerous weapon in her hand?'

'I don't know,' Serena said, sinking into depression again. 'It was inexcusable, wasn't it?'

'To put it mildly, although possibly you have the excuse ready?'

'I must have been mad, that's the best I can think of. It's been such an awful time, I've hardly slept at all and that made me even more confused. Everything seemed to go from bad to worse and I didn't dare imagine where it might end. It frightened me so much that I was half out of my mind.'

'Not bad,' Robin conceded, 'but I doubt if it would get you far in a criminal court. You still haven't explained how you came to be so confused as to regard Tessa as your enemy.'

'I hadn't, but I was afraid, was sure in fact, that she'd found out the whole dismal truth.'

'Ah!'

'Don't say "Ah" in that tone, Robin. I know very well what it implies, but you're wrong. I only wanted to try and persuade her to keep quiet for my sake. I had somehow to make her understand that it had all been my fault and that I was prepared to pay for it for the rest of my life; that it would be the reverse of justice if there were to be a trial.'

'And if you had failed to convince her, which seems rather likely on the face of it?'

'Well yes, I suppose I must admit it. If I had failed I really did have some crazy idea of using the knife as a threat, pretending I would scar her face, so that she could never act again, or something equally terrible,' Serena moaned, covering her eyes with her hands. 'It's too degrading to be borne, but you have my solemn word that I would never have carried it out. It was only a threat, because I was so desperate.'

'Yes, I believe you,' I said again.

'To be fair, so do I,' Robin admitted. 'Oh yes, Serena, you've done it again. The fact is you could have invented a perfectly plausible excuse for being on the attic floor with a knife, if you weren't so damned truthful. You had only to claim that you'd heard a man's voice, feared Tessa might be in danger and were trying to protect her. The trouble with you is that your lies take the form of omissions, rather than inventions, and you're not even very clever about those.'

Serena's expression reflected a strong desire to declare that she had not come here to be insulted, but evidently realising that such an attitude would be untenable, quickly changed it to one of resignation.

'I know. I'm not particularly deceitful by nature and I hate having to lie. The role has been forced on me.'

'Ever since the Thorne boy died?'

She nodded: 'Almost twenty years ago. You'd think I'd have got better at it by now.'

'You knew from the beginning who was responsible?'

'No, although I had the most agonising doubts. It wasn't until Primrose started getting nightmares and talking in her sleep that the truth dawned on us and Nannie and I made a pact never to reveal it to anyone. I was terrified, as you can imagine; terrified to think what sort of monster I had given birth to, terrified of Nannie's new hold over us, but terrified most of all that the truth would leak out and we should all be cruelly punished.'

'Might that not have been better in the end? She could have had psychiatric treatment and got the demons exorcised.'

Serena shook her head: 'I don't know, Robin. I expect you're right, events have proved that you are, but it's no use asking me questions like that now. One does what one thinks is best at the time and that's all there is to it. I suppose I had pinned my hopes on the demons being pushed out of sight until they were buried and forgotten. She was very young, you know, only six years old and the memory might have faded, just as the nightmares did. Besides, it wasn't only ourselves I was thinking of, there was Rupert too. In a way, it would have been like defiling his memory if it had come out that his child had behaved in such a sadistic way.'

'Weren't you afraid she might do it again, to some other child?' I asked.

'No, Alan was a unique case, and so was the provocation. When I spoke of her being a monster, I was giving you the worst construction; there is another, more presentable side to the medal. I've told you already that Alan was a thoroughly nasty child and whenever he knew for certain that neither his mother nor Nannie could hear he used to tease Primrose unmercifully. I knew it and I should have put a stop to it, along with all the other things I should have done, but she was so cut off from other children that I persuaded myself that even this companionship was healthier than none at all. However, there was another element, far more serious which, God help me, I was never aware of until she started having those bad dreams.'

'He had told her who his father was?' I suggested.

'Yes, or rather the version which was popularly accepted. He was a year or two older than her, you see, and bright, in spite of being so small and spindly, and along with all the other half truths he'd picked up some distorted facts about the entail. Evidently he had taunted her with them, saying that when they grew up he would be the master of the big house and she would be his slave. Being slow witted and inarticulate, she was no match for him with words.'

'So she hit back with deeds,' Robin said, making it a statement, not a question.

'Yes, and I don't pretend that anything excuses it, but you must hear all the facts before you condemn her utterly. You see, I am positive that tying Alan to the tree started simply as a prank, to pay him out for tormenting her, and that she fully intended to release him when it came to his dinner time. Unfortunately, Nannie caught up with her in the interval and after that she never let Primrose out of her sight until we set off for the party. And you'll remember that when we arrived there it was fixed that they should both stay the night. I am convinced to this day that if we had all returned that evening, as planned and learnt that Alan was missing, Primrose would have owned up and he would have suffered nothing worse than a bad cold and a bad fright. But, in fact, our kind hosts insisted on keeping her with them until after the funeral. Everyone was so intent on sparing her feelings that not a word was breathed about Alan in her hearing and, personally, I am certain that if she remembered the incident at all she believed that he had been found and was safe and well. When she came home and, little by little, discovered the truth, she must have been demented with fear and it has warped her to this day. That is my firm belief and nothing you can say will shake me out of it.'

Robin said: 'We shan't try to, Serena. I can understand your feelings and why you felt justified in acting as you did, but surely even you would not pretend that you can keep it up, now that two more people have died?'

'I suppose I must have thought so,' she replied helplessly. 'It just shows how crazy I've become. Secretly, you know, I've always believed that if there was a streak of insanity or cruelty in Primrose, it must have come from Rupert's family. Pelham used to behave so strangely at times. But perhaps, after all, she got it from me.'

'Apart from moral scruples, did you seriously hope to get away with it?'

Serena glanced at me briefly before answering: 'The ironic thing is, Robin, that I might have succeeded, if it hadn't been for . . .'

'Tessa?'

She nodded: 'I set out to use her, and then to deceive her, and it resulted in arousing her curiosity to the point where it rebounded on myself. At first, I wasn't worried because it never occurred to me that she could conceive of a motive for Primrose killing Nannie, whom she so loved and adored, and when it came to Lindy's turn I was terribly afraid, but you were both so confident that it would be called suicide that I began to feel almost secure. I still don't understand how it all went wrong.'

'The final proof has yet to come,' I told her, 'and, strangely enough, if and when it does, it will only be in a negative form.'

'That makes it even more mystifying.'

'There was a letter, you see, or rather two to be precise, and they were left in the box on the night before Lindy died. One was from me to Robin and it never reached him. The second was an airmail letter to a doctor in California, but it will be weeks before we can say positively that it wasn't posted, because it was under-stamped and would have been sent by surface mail. The chances are, though, that they were both removed by Primrose hours before the post-man called here. My own letter contained evidence which might have been damaging, or at any rate indicated that I was on her trail. When Robin and I grasped what had become of it we thought she might possibly have marked me down as the next to go, which is why he happened to be so conveniently parked in the drive this evening. He was waiting for some flashing lights.'

'How dreadful! I do wish you'd told me. You must have known that I wouldn't have kept quiet if you were in danger?'

'No, I'm sure you wouldn't, but no doubt your first instinct would have been to warn Primrose that the trap was baited and that wouldn't have done any good at all.'

'I suppose there's no use denying it. To be honest, I can't tell you what I might have done. How about the other letter, though? Why would she have wanted that?'

'Perhaps simply on the principle of leaving no stone unturned; perhaps, like me, she noticed the stamp and was afraid the postman would notice too. That could have led to awkward questions about the other letter, so on the whole it was safer to take them both and, in fact, Lindy's turned out to be a far greater windfall.'

'Yes, I begin to follow you.'

'It was written, you see, when the poor girl was in a fearful panic, before Dr Soames got at her and changed it all to lollipops and roses. In the meantime, she'd most likely taken a lot of sedative pills, which always made her muzzy and forgetful, so she didn't even remember having written the letter and left it in the box. It was a real bonus for Primrose though, because the handwriting was all wild and uneven and the words not only threatened suicide, but gave the reason. It only needed to remove a page from the middle, place it on Lindy's dressing table and destroy the rest. The single tricky part was in the timing, where she showed real nerve. As far as we can see, she must have planted it when the hunt was already on; in other words, after she had joined Lindy on her afternoon walk, taken her up to High Copse and put a bullet into her and then returned here. She was taking one hell of a chance because the room might already have been searched, for all she knew, but in fact she got away with it.'

Serena nodded: 'And of course there wasn't such a tremendous risk, was there? When someone vanishes, you don't normally waste time combing through their bedroom. You assume they have wandered off out of doors, which is exactly what we all did. What I find more puzzling is how Primrose managed to entice her to that place. What pretext can she have used?'

'No pretext,' I said, 'and no enticement. Lindy was dead keen to go there and undoubtedly was the one to propose it. She had a morbid desire to see for herself where the boy had been tied up. She was quite proud of it, believe it or not, and she once tried to get me to go there with her.

That didn't come off though, and my guess is that her next move was to get round Primrose to take her. Poor girl, she practically asked to be murdered.'

'Yes, and doesn't it make one suspect that she really was insane? Either that or the death wish was stronger than anyone realised? How could she have been so idiotic as to go off alone with Primrose, knowing what she did?'

'And precisely what did she know, Serena?' Robin asked.

'That Primrose was responsible for Nannie's death, presumably.'

'Oh, dear me, no, nothing of the kind.'

'We think Lindy had stumbled on part of the story,' I explained, 'but she'd got it mixed up. She actually tried to give me a hint on one occasion and I could have acted on it sooner, if only I'd known what she was driving at.'

'I don't understand. A hint of what?'

'That Jake might have murdered Nannie.'

'But how absurd! What could have given her such an extraordinary idea?'

'Something she'd overheard; hence tonight's experiment. Do you remember how ill Lindy was on the night Nannie died?'

'As though one could ever forget!'

'It's probable that she'd swallowed some rat poison herself, on top of all her other troubles, because Primrose had doctored the sugar, to ensure that other people would have a few of the symptoms. When I ran into Lindy, on my way to break the news, she was creeping out of the bathroom and she told me it was the third time she'd been sick. I saw the significance of it this evening, when Pelham pointed out the shortage of plumbing amenities. Everyone knows that when a person feels violently ill they don't hang around politely waiting for the nearest bathroom to become vacant, they make a dash for another one, in this case the only other one. I'll bet you anything that during at least one of her earlier attacks she had gone up to the top bathroom and was there while Primrose and Nannie were talking in the nursery.'

'I still don't see how Jake comes into it.'

'Well, the point is, Serena, when the attics were converted they put up these thin partition walls, with the result that I could hear every word of my driving lesson tonight, without even straining. You wouldn't expect non-pros to come through quite so clearly, but although Nannie had become faint and querulous in her old age, we are all aware that Primrose booms out like a foghorn. According to my theory, Jake and Primrose had made the final plans for wedding bells during their Newmarket trip. She was looking as jolly as a sandboy when she came back and she took more trouble over her appearance that evening, when Jake dined with us, than anyone had ever seen before. The rather sad thing is that if all had gone along smoothly from that point she might gradually have developed into quite a good natured, civilised human being.'

'I agree and it does seem so cruel that she should have to suffer for something which happened so long ago.'

'Lindy and Nannie suffered a bit too, Serena,' Robin reminded her.

'There's no point in going over all that,' I said, 'because, nothing ever did go smoothly and never could have, so long as Nannie lived. Knowing Primrose as we do, it practically goes without saying that she would have told Nannie, before anyone else, what she and Jake were planning, and of course the reception was far from rapturous. Nannie would have been dead against it and I believe that Primrose had discovered this and had already taken steps, before the

Newmarket trip, to put the old woman out of the way; not to mention hiding her glasses to make the incidence of rat poison more plausible in the event of a medical enquiry. I don't know whether she put them in the spare room with some vague idea of incriminating Pelham, bur I daresay it was while she was looking round for a hiding place that she came across his gun. What she didn't know was that Nannie had already been taking a regular supply of Warfarin and that a much larger dose would be needed to do the trick than she had bargained for. Anyway, it must have been a nasty jolt when she returned from Newmarket to find the old girl just as bobbish as ever and just as adamant. I think that's what put her into such a sulk at dinner and why she flounced upstairs and refused to come down again.

'Nannie really loved Primrose,' I went on, looking squarely at Serena, 'so, unlike you, she never had to pretend that her faults sprang from shyness or immaturity, or any of those other comforting little euphemisms. Nannie recognised her faults and loved her in spite of them, but she was a puritan minded old party and she knew all about the family heritage. She knew or guessed, as you did no doubt, that Pelham had shot his brother in a fit of rage or jealousy, that as a young man Rupert had felt no qualms about frightening a small child out of its wits by dressing up as a wild animal, and she also knew what Primrose had done to Alan. Above all, she knew that it would be wrong for her to marry and have children of her own. Am I right?'

'What can I say? As you know, I never believed that tale about Rupert and if it's true I'm sure it was only a joke that misfired, but Nan was certainly a great bible thumper and always on about the sins of the father and so forth, I can't dispute that.'

'Although one couldn't expect Primrose to see it in the same light. She would have disputed at the top of her lungs.'

'And you're suggesting that Lindy heard them arguing about it?'

'No, I think what she heard was one side of an argument, that is every syllable from Primrose, just indistinct murmurs from Nannie. Something like this, for example,' I said, switching to an imitation of Primrose at her most stentorian. '"But that wasn't murder, you old fool, that was an accident and anyway it was all over and done with ages ago. I'm not going to let a silly thing like that spoil my life, so don't you dare interfere. If you do, I'm warning you, I'll tell Jake and he'll bloody well kill you."

'Well, something to that effect,' I amended, reverting to normal speech. 'Naturally, I can't give you the exact words, but you can picture the scene and Lindy, who hadn't the faintest interest in Chargrove history, would have concluded that Nannie had heard about the rather shady story of Jake's former wife and was warning Primrose off him, instead of the other way round.'

'How could she have heard about it, my dear? Even Lindy could have guessed that Hollywood was as remote to her as the moon and that kind of gossip quite out of her sphere.'

'On the other hand, there were two known facts for her to work from. One was that Pelham could have told Nannie about it because he was in Santa Barbara himself at the time. Lindy also knew, because he said so in her presence, that Jake was in the habit of going up to the nursery for a chat and therefore Nannie could have formed her own opinions of his rackety past and low moral standards. She wouldn't have been so far off the mark in assessing this as the last set up Nannie would have wished for her darling girl.'

'So you've assumed that Primrose realised she'd been overheard and made up her mind to kill Lindy as soon as she got the chance?'

'No, you go too fast. What probably happened is that when she came out of the nursery, having administered that massive lethal dose, the natural inclination would have been to wash any traces of it off her hands and she got a bad shock when she found the bathroom was occupied. Without doubt, she concluded that I was the occupant, which was why she searched my room, for she knows all about my trick of writing down the things I specially need to remember. She didn't find any record of that conversation among my possessions, although there was another message there, which she thought it better to remove. There was no reference to it in my letter to Robin either, which was when I was doubtless relegated to the rank of public enemy number two. I don't know how she eventually arrived at Lindy as the main risk, but it could have been simply by putting two and two together, or maybe poor ingenuous Lindy gave it away herself. Anyway, when she asked Primrose to show her where that poor little boy had been tied to a tree in a blizzard, and to make it a big secret between them, her number was really up. She'd handed in her life on a plate.'

There followed a prolonged silence, in which Serena leaned forward over the table and fiddled with the handle of the carving knife. I wasn't seriously alarmed, however, and in fact she dropped it back on the table before looking up at us with a slight grimace, as she said:

'Yes, you have made it all very clear; one might say devastatingly clear, and I suppose there is nothing on earth I can say to persuade you to stop the wheels turn-ing? I would so much rather, you know, if only it could be arranged, I would so much rather be the one to be tried and sent to prison. I mean that sincerely.'

Robin shook his head: 'You must know you are talk-ing nonsense, Serena, and even if it sounds like sense to you now, you surely know that I couldn't be part of such a conspiracy?'

'So what comes next?'

'I'm afraid I must telephone the Superintendent. I expect he will decide to come out here tonight, but if so there is no need for you to be present. I suggest that you go to your room now and stay there with Tessa until you are needed.'

She bowed her head and rose at once, without further protest. The fight had gone out of her and she looked passive and resigned. She had cause to be too, for in a sense the last laugh was on us. Primrose was not in her room; nor did she return to West Lodge on that or any other night. She had taken her passport and enough clothes to fill a small suitcase, and so perhaps after all Serena's motive in choosing the kitchen as a conference room had differed from ours. It was out of sight of the hall and Primrose could have walked out practically under our noses. There was no warrant out for her arrest, so no one could have prevented her leaving the country, and she vanished just as effectively as Pelham had twenty-five years before. Perhaps she is leading a harmless and useful life somewhere, looking after dogs or horses and, if so, I daresay they will be quite safe in her hands, for she always preferred animals to people.

I have never quite been able to make up my mind whether Robin was a jump or two ahead of me during that memorable discussion round the kitchen table and whether, despite his stern, self-righteous claim at the end of it, he half sensed that the guilty one was getting clean away. Unfortunately, he is a very poor liar, so it would be unfair to ask him.

THE END

FELICITY SHAW

THE detective novels of Anne Morice seem rather to reflect the actual life and background of the author, whose full married name was Felicity Anne Morice Worthington Shaw. Felicity was born in the county of Kent on February 18, 1916, one of four daughters of Harry Edward Worthington, a well-loved village doctor, and his pretty young wife, Muriel Rose Morice. Seemingly this is an unexceptional provenance for an English mystery writer—yet in fact Felicity's complicated ancestry was like something out of a classic English mystery, with several cases of children born on the wrong side of the blanket to prominent sires and their humbly born paramours. Her mother Muriel Rose was the natural daughter of dressmaker Rebecca Garnett Gould and Charles John Morice, a Harrow graduate and footballer who played in the 1872 England/Scotland match. Doffing his football kit after this triumph, Charles became a stockbroker like his father, his brothers and his nephew Percy John de Paravicini, son of Baron James Prior de Paravicini and Charles' only surviving sister, Valentina Antoinette Sampayo Morice. (Of Scottish mercantile origin, the Morices had extensive Portuguese business connections.) Charles also found time, when not playing the fields of sport or commerce, to father a pair of out-of-wedlock children with a coachman's daughter, Clementina Frances Turvey, whom he would later marry.

Her mother having passed away when she was only four years old, Muriel Rose was raised by her half-sister Kitty, who had wed a commercial traveler, at the village of Birchington-on-Sea, Kent, near the city of Margate. There she met kindly local doctor Harry Worthington when he treated her during a local measles outbreak.

The case of measles led to marriage between the physician and his patient, with the couple wedding in 1904, when Harry was thirty-six and Muriel Rose but twenty-two. Together Harry and Muriel Rose had a daughter, Elizabeth, in 1906. However Muriel Rose's three later daughters—Angela, Felicity and Yvonne—were fathered by another man, London playwright Frederick Leonard Lonsdale, the author of such popular stage works (many of them adapted as films) as *On Approval* and *The Last of Mrs. Cheyney* as well as being the most steady of Muriel Rose's many lovers.

Unfortunately for Muriel Rose, Lonsdale's interest in her evaporated as his stage success mounted. The playwright proposed pensioning off his discarded mistress with an annual stipend of one hundred pounds apiece for each of his natural daughters, provided that he and Muriel Rose never met again. The offer was accepted, although Muriel Rose, a woman of golden flights and fancies who romantically went by the name Lucy Glitters (she told her daughters that her father had christened her with this appellation on account of his having won a bet on a horse by that name on the day she was born), never got over the rejection. Meanwhile, "poor Dr. Worthington" as he was now known, had come down with Parkinson's Disease and he was packed off with a nurse to a cottage while "Lucy Glitters," now in straitened financial circumstances by her standards, moved with her daughters to a maisonette above a cake shop in Belgravia, London, in a bid to get the girls established. Felicity's older sister Angela went into acting for a profession, and her mother's theatrical ambition for her daughter is said to have been the inspiration for Noel Coward's amusingly imploring 1935 hit song "Don't Put Your Daughter on the Stage, Mrs. Worthington." Angela's greatest contribution to the cause of thespianism by far came when she married actor and theatrical agent Robin Fox, with whom she produced England's Fox acting dynasty, including her sons Edward and James and grandchildren Laurence, Jack, Emilia and Freddie.

Felicity meanwhile went to work in the office of the GPO Film Unit, a subdivision of the United Kingdom's General Post Office established in 1933 to produce documentary films. Her daughter Mary Premila Boseman has written that it was at the GPO Film Unit that the "pretty and fashionably slim" Felicity met documentarian Alexander Shaw—"good looking, strong featured, dark haired and with strange brown eyes between yellow and green"— and told herself "that's the man I'm going to marry," which she did. During the Thirties and Forties Alex produced and/or directed over a score of prestige documentaries, including *Tank Patrol*, *Our Country* (introduced by actor Burgess Meredith) and *Penicillin*. After World War Two Alex worked with the United Nations agencies UNESCO and UNRWA and he and Felicity and their three children resided in developing nations all around the world. Felicity's daughter Mary recalls that Felicity "set up house in most of these places adapting to each circumstance. Furniture and curtains and so on were made of local materials. ... The only possession that followed us everywhere from England was the box of Christmas decorations, practically heirlooms, fragile and attractive and unbroken throughout. In Wad Medani in the Sudan they hung on a thorn bush and looked charming."

It was during these years that Felicity began writing fiction, eventually publishing two fine mainstream novels, *The Happy Exiles* (1956) and *Sun-Trap* (1958). The former novel, a lightly satirical comedy of manners about British and American expatriates in an unnamed British colony during the dying days of the Empire, received particularly good reviews and was published in both the United Kingdom and the United States, but after a nasty bout with malaria and the death, back in England, of her mother Lucy Glitters, Felicity put writing aside for more than a decade, until under her pseudonym Anne Morice, drawn from her two middle names, she successfully launched her Tessa Crichton mystery series in 1970. "From the royalties of these books," notes Mary Premila Boseman, "she was able to buy a house in Hambleden, near Henley-on-Thames; this was the first of our houses that wasn't rented." Felicity spent a great deal more time in the home country during the last two decades of her life, gardening and cooking for friends (though she herself when alone subsisted on a diet of black coffee and watercress) and industriously spinning her tales of genteel English murder in locales much like that in which she now resided. Sometimes she joined Alex in his overseas travels to different places, including Washington, D.C., which she wrote about with characteristic wryness in her 1977 detective novel *Murder with Mimicry* ("a nice lively book saturated with show business," pronounced the *New York Times Book Review*). Felicity Shaw lived a full life of richly varied experiences, which are rewardingly reflected in her books, the last of which was published posthumously in 1990, a year after her death at the age of seventy-three on May 18th, 1989.

Curtis Evans